Crime of Passion

Lock Down Publications and Ca$h
Presents

Crime of Passion

A Novel by *Mimi*

Lock Down Publications

P.O. Box 870494
Mesquite, Tx 75187

Visit our website @
www.lockdownpublications.com

Copyright 2018 by Crime of Passion

First Edition September 2018
Printed in the United States of America

This is a work of fiction. Names, characters, places, and incidents either are products of the author's imagination or are used fictitiously. Any similarity to actual events or locales or persons, living or dead, is entirely coincidental.

Lock Down Publications
Like our page on Facebook: Lock Down Publications @
www.facebook.com/lockdownpublications.ldp
Cover design and layout by: **Dynasty Cover Me**
Book interior design by: **Shawn Walker**
Edited by: **Lashonda Johnson**

Stay Connected with Us!

Text **LOCKDOWN** to 22828 to stay up-to-date with new releases, sneak peaks, contests and more…
Thank you.

Warning This material may cause triggers, as it has to deal with domestic violence.

~Dedication~

Writing this book took me on a journey. Not many people know that I was in a domestic violence relationship and while none of this, in this book is what I went through, I know that it may be true for most. I want to dedicate this book to all the domestic violence survivors and to the women who may still be going through it. Most times we feel like there is no way to leave but I'm telling you that YOU can and that it is OKAY to LEAVE! You are not alone!

To my readers thank you for giving me the opportunity to allow me to deliver you some heat! I work extremely hard and work my fingers to the bone to give you nothing but the best.

To my LDP fam, thank ya'll for always holding it down and supporting me from the gate! It's an LDP thang, baby, and I look forward to growing with all ya'll!

XoXo

MIMI

Introduction

Only God knows where the story is
For me, but I know where the story begins
It's up to us to choose
Whatever we win or lose
And I choose to win

Flashes of the past two hours ran through my mind. My white, porcelain, claw-foot tub held scorching hot water, awaiting my descend. I looked around the all-white bathroom, and my eyes connected with the circular mirror, I had avoided for so many months. Slowly, my eyes began to wander up and settled on the person looking back at me. I didn't recognize her. My once flawless, light-honey colored skin was free from the foundation, I used daily to cover up the scars.

My eyes were swollen and bruised from the constant abuse, I had suffered for the past two hours. Though that didn't compare to the constant abuse, I'd experienced over the last few months. My lip was busted so bad it was split on the top and bottom. There was blood draining from my ear, down my face, and onto my shoulder. My hair, my thick, beautiful hair was now extremely thin due to stress and tossed around on my head.

If you would have asked me if I knew this was going to happen, I would have said no. In fact, I was outright angry at myself for allowing this to happen. As I looked in the mirror, I forced myself to wipe the tears from my eyes, deciding now was the perfect time to stop feeling sorry for myself. I took off the terry cloth robe, I saw new black and blue bruises along with the yellow discoloration from the old ones. Tears threatened to fall from my eyes, but I wouldn't allow them to do so.

For years I cried, today was the day, I stopped and stood strong. Finally, turning from the mirror, I walked over to the tub and one foot at a time, I slid in. The water sloshed around my body threatening to spill over, but it immediately soothed my aching body. In flashes, I remembered the backhanded slap I received from Jason, the pain from the punch that landed to my stomach, and the words, *"You, worthless piece of shit!"* rang through my head. I shut my eyes as tight as I could to get rid of those thoughts. The room was silent, so silent, I couldn't bear it.

The sound of heels clicking across the marbled, tiled floors outside of the bathroom caught my attention. My ears perked up as I listened to the high heels crackle over the glass that lined the floor in the hallway. My best friend of seventeen years entered the bathroom. Her mouth was agape, and her eyes bugged out of her head once she laid her eyes on me. I stared back at her with the silence that needed to happen. I knew she couldn't believe the severity of the issue at hand, and she was in complete utter shock. Slowly, Erica began walking towards me and sat down on the toilet.

"Quinn, baby girl, what happened?" Erica asked.

It was obvious what had happened, but I guess when you are in shock, you ask the obvious.

I looked at Erica, exhaled through the pain I felt in my ribs, and said, "I ended a cycle."

Chapter One

*I mean shit he bought you things and gave you diamond
rings
But them things wasn't worth none of the pain that he
brings
And you stayed, what made you fall for him
That nigga had the power to make you crawl for him*

~In the Beginning~

The lights over the vanity where my mother was sitting, illuminated against her skin. I sat on the floor next to her, watching her apply make-up to her face. Since I could remember, my mother would apply make-up to her face, after her and my father got into arguments. At this present time, I was only about eight, but she'd been doing this since I was three. I looked up just at the right time to catch the tears sliding down my mother's face, as she tried to wipe them away. My mother caught my reflection looking at her, and gave me a weak smile. I remember asking her why she always wore makeup if she was already beautiful. Beautiful was just an understatement of how my mother looked.

My mother, Giselle Elise Boyd was mulatto. She had light skin, with an oval-shaped face. Her lips were medium-full and deep dimples sat on each cheek. Her cheekbones sat up high and were well-defined. My mother had thick, wavy, brown hair that she always wore in a long braid down her back. She also had freckles across the bridge of her nose, but she always hid them under makeup.

I looked at my mother again and asked, "Mommy, if you are already beautiful, why do you need makeup?"

9

"Sweetheart, it's for mommy to look even more beautiful than what she is. There is nothing wrong with enhancing your beauty dear," she answered.

In my little eight-year-old mind, I didn't think much of it. When I got a tad bit older, I knew what she meant by it. I grabbed my doll and left out of my parent's room. Daddy would be home soon, and he didn't like his children inside of their room. I went to search for my brother, Donald. He was in our backyard playing with our dog, Izzy. I sat down on the grass and watched as Donald and Izzy ran back and forth across the grass.

About ten minutes passed before Donald and I realized Daddy was home from work. Ernest Cornell Boyd the owner of Boyd Construction, was my father. He was African-American, had a perfect circular face, with a defined, slightly pointed chin and a sturdy jawline. His dark eyes were big and spaced evenly apart under bushy eyebrows that seemed to curve as a natural extension of his broad, rounded nose. For as long as I could remember, daddy had been bald, with a neatly trimmed mustache and beard which had little sprinkles of grey in it. He was six-foot-four to be exact, and his physique was like a football player's.

Donald and I made our way inside the house to get cleaned up for dinner, while mom set the table. I was surprised she didn't have the table already set. When we entered the kitchen, we took our seats and waited for mom to finish setting the table. Daddy placed a jewelry box on the table where mommy sat. I knew, he was apologizing for beating on her the night before. He then slid me the same colored box, just smaller and winked at me.

Everything he gifted to momma he gave to me, and I was always content. Donald on the other hand, he disliked our father because at the time he knew what Daddy was doing to mommy, and he didn't like it. I knew too, but all was forgiven once I received whatever gift was being given. I heard Donald mumble something under his breath and watched as Daddy eyed him.

"Is my family ready to eat?" My mother asked with the brightest smile on her face.

My father looked up at my mother in admiration, as he stood to give her a kiss on her lips. Her smile faded just a tad bit until she noticed I was watching. Her smile brightened again, and she began to fix daddy's food before ours. All was well in the Boyd household. At least for now.

I had gotten up in the middle of the night to use the bathroom, but the muffled noises of my parents piqued my interest, and I began walking to their room. I could hear them arguing about something, then I heard a loud thump. I was curious and wanted to know what was going on, so I opened the door just enough to see inside the room. My mother was on the floor, dragging her body away from my dad, as he towered over her in a stalking manner. He jumped on top of her and backhanded her, causing her head to almost spin around in a full circle.

"It's your fault that boy doesn't respect me," I heard my daddy hiss.

My mouth hung open as my little eight-year-old eyes watched my daddy attack my mother. I knew this was going on, but to see it happening in front of me had me stuck.

"Ernest, I didn't turn him against you. He loves you," my mother whimpered.

She was holding her face while defending her only boy. Everyone in the house knew Donald had a strong dislike for daddy, and it wasn't a secret that most of the time, mommy and daddy's fights were about Donald.

"He's probably not even my son," Daddy said as he raised his hand, and smacked mom across the face twice, then punched her in the cheek and nose.

Her hand instinctively, went to her nose to stop the gush of blood that flew from it. The blood didn't stop *daddy, though. He proceeded to grin and wrap his fingers around mommy's neck. I felt the hot tears cascade down my face as me and mommy made eye contact, and she mouthed for me to dial 911.*

***

I woke up gasping for air like it was me who was being choked. These dreams I was having had become frequent and I found myself waking up in a cold sweat at least four times out of the week. I sat up in my bed and reached for my phone to see what time it was. The clock read six-forty-five. Now was the best time to start getting ready for my eight-o-clock appointment down at the welfare office. The welfare office was the one place, I didn't want to spend my day since it was going to be nice out, and I knew I was going to be there the whole day. I walked to my kitchen to put on some coffee and made my way to the bathroom.

The small bathroom was big enough just for the sink, toilet, and bathtub. I had a full-length body mirror hanging from the back of the door. I stripped out of my damp pajama shorts and the matching tank top. I looked at myself in the mirror and was satisfied with what I saw. I stood five-feet-eight inches, my skin was scar and blemish free. I had gotten my light-skin from my mother, who was black and white. I had inherited grey eyes from her side of the family and my body from my dad's side of the family. I had an hourglass shape of thirty-eight, twenty-four, forty. I loved my body.

My mother also passed down her thick, wavy hair to me, which was hard to tame. I understood why she would always wear it in a braid down her back. I was drop dead gorgeous and had to give thanks to my mother. After I admired myself, I stood under the steaming hot water of my shower and stood there. I said my daily prayers and began lathering my wash rag with lavender vanilla body wash, my favorite scent from *'Bath and Body Works'*. Not too long after, I got out and smoothed *'Palmer's Cocoa Butter'* lotion all over my body and got dressed.

I wore a pair of blue jean shorts that stopped right above my knee and a red tank top with *'I Woke Up Like This #Flawless'* written in gold on the front. On my feet, I rocked my white Old Navy Skippy's and grabbed my purse with my belongings. As I headed out the door, my cell phone began ringing. I knew it was my best friend, Erica.

"What do you want, trick? Why are you calling my phone so early this morning?" I said.

Erica yawned and said, "What are you doing?"

"I have to go down to the welfare office. They want to cut me off because I missed an appointment. Well at least, that's what they are going by. I've been to every appointment they assigned me," I explained stepping into the hot sun. It wasn't even eight yet and the sun was scorching. *These fools better be lucky, I need these benefits. I would turn my ass right around and go inside my air-conditioned apartment,'* I thought silently to myself.

Erica asked, "Shit, what time is it? I have to go down there too, to bring some papers."

"It's almost eight, but you need to come on. I got an eight-o-clock appointment, so I'll meet you down there," I said.

"A'ight, here I come."

We hung up and I made my way to the welfare office. I was glad, I had an early appointment because even though, they would take forever to get to me. I knew I'd still be out in just enough time for lunch. Going to welfare was something I despised, if I didn't need them, I swear I wouldn't go. Who am I lying, too? Free food stamps, you can't beat it. I needed a job soon, though, because they were using that also to threaten to cut me off. I made it to the Department of Social Services ten minutes before eight and hurriedly got in line to check in. I looked around at all the people that were there. Some of them were always there for one thing or another.

The welfare building was like their living quarters. I didn't understand it. After I was checked in, I took my seat and got comfortable for the long wait. Not too long after, I noticed Erica enter and walk up to the window. She handed her papers over to the clerk and headed my way. She took her seat next to me and fanned herself.

She said, "It's always so damn hot in here like they don't have money to fix this air conditioning. You look cute."

"Thank you, and you hot because you were rushing through the doors. Give it some time, you will cool down," I said hoping they would call me soon. Erica was already done and I wanted out of that place.

"Quinn Boyd," I heard my name yelled after an hour of waiting.

I walked to the door and waited for them to let me in. I was in the back for five minutes, just long enough for them to say they'd made a mistake and would fix the paperwork so I could continue getting my benefits.

My face twisted up when this fat, white, bitch said that, "For all of that, we could have done this over the phone."

I walked out and signaled for Erica to come on. When we were outside, I told her what happened, and we began walking towards downtown Schenectady.

"Girl, there is this party going down tonight. Are you down?" Erica asked being quite animated.

"Where is this party? I'm tired of going to parties with you," I stated.

Erica laughed and said, "What do you mean, you're tired of going to parties with me?"

"You know exactly what I'm talking about. That's why you're laughing." I couldn't help but join in with her laughter.

The last time I went to a party with Erica we had to climb out of the window and go down somebody's fire escape. The police came busting through the door looking for somebody and the only way we were going to get out of that party, without a bullet to the back of our heads was to go down the fire escape. That wasn't even the half of it though, we were almost involved in a stampede because so many people were trying to get away, too. I cracked up at the thought.

"I have apologized so many times for that. Are you going to hold that over my head for forever?" She asked, holding her stomach trying to control her laughter.

"I almost died that night. So, if you gonna apologize, you're going to be apologizing forever," I said, cracking up at my best *Cardi-B* impersonation.

Erica had to stop walking she was laughing so hard. We finally made it to our destination, which was Subway on State Street. We ordered our food and took our seats. We began eating and Erica began telling me about this guy she was dealing with. My attention wasn't on her for too long, because four guys dressed in Army uniforms entered the Subway. I made eye contact with one of them, and he flashed a smile full of white teeth. I almost melted in my seat. I checked him out from head to toe once he walked passed me and up to the counter.

One of his army friends said something funny and he threw his head back in laughter. He had to have been six-foot-five, almost two hundred pounds, milk-chocolate skin with a few blemishes, chinky shaped eyes and a squared chin with a dimple in the middle of it. He was clean shaved, and his jawline was strong. I couldn't tell if he had hair or not because his army fatigue hat covered his head. He was muscular and slightly bow-legged. I took a sip of my drink wishing it was him.

"Hello, earth to, Quinn," Erica said, snapping her fingers in front of my face.

"Huh," I replied, blushing because he'd looked in my direction.

"You alright?" She asked, peeking behind her to see what I was looking at.

"Yes, I'm A-Okay now," I responded.

Erica cracked a smile and leaned in towards me. "Girl, he is cute, you should go scoop him."

"He is fine and all, but I'll pass."

Erica's eyes got as big as saucers. "What? Why would you pass on that?"

"Because a guy that fine must be either married, has a girlfriend, or is gay. I don't have time to figure that thing out. Come on let's just finish eating so we can go," I said, now rushing to finish my sandwich.

The guy who I was ogling and did all but marry his ass in my head started making his way towards our table. His eyes were trained on me and his teeth were shining brightly. My palms were sweaty by the time he reached me. He reached his hand out, I wiped my hand on my napkin, and allowed for my dainty hand to be swallowed by his.

"Hi, my name is Jason, I couldn't help but notice how beautiful you are. I was just telling my buddies, I couldn't leave without at least getting your name," he said with a smile.

I guess I took too long to respond and Erica kicked me under the table.

"Oh, um, I'm sorry about that, I'm Quinn. It's nice to meet you." I managed to get out. *'Girl, what is wrong with you? You don't sweat men like that,'* I pep talked myself.

"Feelings mutual. If it's okay, can I leave you with my number? Maybe one day, we can have dinner and get to know each other."

"Sure, you can put your number in my phone," I responded and passed Jason my cell phone. I watched as he programmed his number in my phone and handed it back to me.

"Give me a call sometime soon. It was nice meeting you beautiful." He shook my hand one last time, then raised my hand to his lips and kissed the back of it. Lastly, he winked his eye, returned to his Army buddies and exited out of Subway.

I couldn't take my eyes off the door until I caught Erica peeking her head under the table.

"Girl, what is wrong with you? What are you doing?" I asked, trying not to laugh at her silliness.

"I'm just trying to make sure you got your panties on still. You drooled so much over that man, I figured you threw your funky ass drawers at him," she cackled.

I threw my napkin at her and said, "Let's go, whore."

Once I left Erica I went home and decided I would take her up on her offer and go to this party. She had assured me it was going to be in Legends, a club out in Albany. She said, she knew the dude who was giving the party and she wanted to go and support him, since he's been supporting her for three years, by putting money in her pocket, and making sure her bills were paid. I looked around my closet to find something to wear, but nothing jumped out at me. I had stripped naked and poured me a glass of Pink Moscato when my phone began to ring. I looked at my phone and noticed it was Lavar calling. A smile spread across my face as I remembered the day, I had met him.

Erica and I had been shoe shopping, and as usual, we were being silly. We decided to get a bite to eat at

17

Wendy's in Crossgates Mall. We got our order and proceeded to take our seats until this dude bumped into me. He almost made me drop my bacon cheeseburger and chocolate Frosty. He immediately started apologizing but I wasn't trying to hear it.

"Fuck your apology! If you would have dropped my food were you going to pay for it?" I asked, grilling him down.

"Miss, I said, I was sorry. You didn't drop your food, so there shouldn't be an issue. I'm not going to keep apologizing."

"Then what are you still standing around for?" I asked, placing my hand on my hip.

He stood there looking like a goofball, I rolled my neck and eyes in every bit of my sister girl glory waiting for his response.

He smiled and said, "Can I get your number?"

I busted out into full laughter. I couldn't believe he had the nerve to ask me for my number after I had just cursed him out. Long story short, I gave him my number and later that night we met up.

I snapped out of my thoughts and picked up the phone before he decided to hang up. I answered, "What's up?"

"You know what's up. I want to come through. You busy?"

"I'm not busy, but I'm stepping out in a few," I responded, browsing my closet again.

"Where are you going?" he asked.

"Erica invited me to go out to this party tonight. If I don't find something to wear, I'm not going."

"I should have known."

I sucked my teeth and said, "You should have known what?"

"That you were going out with that chick," he said it like he had a bad taste in his mouth.

"You make it seem like she is such a bad person. She is not and she's my friend, so watch it," I warned.

"Okay, if you say so. Anyway, I didn't call you to talk about her."

I had a bit of an attitude and didn't want to talk to him anymore. I just wanted him off my line and fast.

I said, "So what did you call me for?"

"I wanted to see you. Hopefully, I can make you change your mind about going out."

"I doubt it don't bother coming. I'll holla at you when I get the time," I responded and hung up.

I didn't know why he didn't like Erica, but it didn't sit well with me. It was like he always had something to say about her and I was through hearing it. I went deeper inside my closet and pulled out a black and white maxi dress. I knew it would cling to my body like a glove. It stopped just below my knee and had a split up to the middle of my thigh. I had forgotten, I'd bought it and was glad I found it. I found my black open toe five-inch stiletto heels with satin bands that laced up my leg. I grabbed some silver jewelry and completed my outfit.

"I should sign my ass up for fashion designing school," I said to myself with laughter.

~Tar Baby~

I heard someone say once, *"If you believe it, you can achieve it."* My goal was to just look like all the other girls. I stood in the mirror staring at all one-hundred and thirty-five pounds of me. My cocoa brown skin glistened from the afternoon's heat, singing loudly into the hairbrush, I was supposed to be using to lay mold my short hair. *"You are beautiful in every single way, words can't bring me down!"* I wanted to believe but I couldn't see it. The reflection looking back at me said the opposite, but still, I kept singing, hoping the words would entrain themselves in my heart and magically, what I saw looking back at me would change.

My daddy always told me, I should never be ashamed of the color of my skin. For it has been kissed by the sun just right for me. Although, it was always a joy to hear him say those things. I couldn't help but wonder what I'd look like if I had lighter skin, longer hair, and hell even bigger breasts.

My mother was a constant reminder that I would never look pretty enough because my skin was darker. I inherited my skin complexion from my daddy and Mom hated it. She was light-skinned and wanted me to be as well. I couldn't help the fact that I had darker skin and when she would call me things like *'Tar Baby'* and *'Porch Monkey'*, I would only wish, I had lighter skin.

'Yes, words can't bring you down. Oh, no, so don't you bring me down today.'

A tear or two slid down my face as I wished only for acceptance from the person who gave birth to me. I hid from her in my room, so I wouldn't have to get badgered by the constant verbal abuse she ever so graciously bestowed upon me daily. My room resembled the way I felt on the inside. Everything was dark. From the curtains to the simple throw rug that laid in front of my dresser that to was black. Nothing about my room screamed happiness and I liked it just so.

"You didn't hear me calling your name, you ugly piece of shit?" I heard my mom yell.

My skin crawled and I cringed when I heard her yelling. I turned to see her standing in the doorway of my room, legs spread shoulder length apart. Her once light pink robe, now dingy and filled with holes was tied loosely around her waist. Her nostrils flared, and her eyes were in thin slits as she gawked at me. I could only imagine what I did now and what other things she would say out of her mouth.

"No, ma'am, I didn't hear you," I said and walked over to my side table to lower the radio down.

"Learn to turn your damn music down, you ugly piece of shit. This isn't nobody's damn club," Mom seethed.

I simply nodded letting her know, I understood. If only she heard my thoughts, I'm pretty sure, she would have beaten me until I was black and blue. She rolled her eyes and walked out of my room, with her hands on her hips never saying what she was calling me for. I'm pretty sure I would pay for it later. *'So, don't you bring me down today!'*

MIMI

Chapter Two

We're living in a fantasy
I feel it when you dance with me
It's feeling like you need to be
My baby, my lady

~Jason~

I couldn't wait until it turned five o'clock. It was a long day at the recruitment center, all I wanted to do was get home, soak in a nice hot bath and have a drink. I'd served six years in combat in Iraq for the U.S Army, now I've been working at the recruitment center for three years. While I didn't like the thought of it at the beginning. I saw the numbers of our young black men dying and figured if there was something I could do to save them, I would. I have come to love my job and wouldn't be happier in any other position.

Since lunchtime, I'd been watching the clock, thinking about the beauty I met in Subway. It had been a while since I'd run into someone so beautiful and was able to draw me to them. I mean she was gorgeous. I'd caught myself several times stopping my paperwork to daydream about, Miss Quinn. This last time, I'd smiled a little too hard when one of my buddies came in my office and looked at me like I'd lost my mind.

"Braxton, you okay?" he asked when he walked in.

"Huh—oh yeah. I was just thinking about something," I answered and shuffled papers around my desk embarrassed.

"Yeah sure. Looks like you were thinking of someone instead of something," he chuckled.

"How can I help you, Daniels?" I asked becoming serious.

I've known Kareem Daniels since I entered the Army. He was my battle buddy and the one who told me about the amazing opportunity to work at the recruitment center. He was like the brother I never had.

"Oh, yeah, the reason I am here is because I wanted to know if you were up to going out for some drinks tonight?" he asked.

"I wish I could, but I have a hot bath and some TiVo waiting on me when I get home."

Daniels screwed up his face and said, "Do you have a pussy between your legs?"

I jumped up out of my seat and peeked my head into the hall. After making sure the coast was clear, I closed my office door and took my seat again.

I said, "First, I shouldn't have to tell you this but I'm going to anyway. We are at work and you need to watch your mouth. Secondly, can't a man just want to relax at home without having to be referred to as a woman. Nowadays, these bars and clubs are filled with young folks. I don't have the time nor the energy to have to beat some young dude's ass because I accidentally stepped on his Jordan's."

"Oh, come on. It's been how long since you been out. Every time I ask if you want to hang, you blow me off for a bath and T.V."

"That's because that's the only thing I'm interested in."

"This one time," Daniels said holding up his index finger.

I looked at Daniels and seriously contemplated about going out. He was right. It had been maybe a year and a half since I'd been out. I think it was a result of being in a four-year relationship, getting engaged, and being left at the altar. I had been in a deep depression for a year. The only thing I did was go to work and go home. I cut all communications off with the world. Marissa had been my everything and she left me at the altar to be with my cousin. They'd been dating each other our whole relationship.

The day we were supposed to wed, was the day she told me the baby she'd been carrying was my cousin's and not mines. She said, she loved and was in love with my cousin, which is why she was choosing him over me. I had questioned if she even loved me to begin with. She said, she did but she never was in love with me the way she was with my cousin. I was heartbroken, to say the least, but when I started to come out of my funk. She called me out of the blue one day and told me how much my cousin was dogging her out.

He told her the baby that was supposed to be his wasn't his. He was cheating on her with different girls from around their way and wasn't providing for his family the way a man is supposed to. Did I feel bad? Not at all, because she started kicking that the baby was possibly mine and she wanted to work on us. I told her I wanted a DNA test and if the baby was mine, I would take care of the baby, but I didn't want to have anything to do with her. She agreed.

We went to a diagnostics center and took the test. I paid five hundred of my own money and waited the six weeks for the test results to come back. Those were the worst stressful six weeks I have ever experienced in my life. When the time came, it turned out that I wasn't the father. I called Daniels and we went and tore the bar up.

"I hope you about to tell me yes for as long as you were quiet," Daniels said causing me to snap out of my thoughts.

"You know what, I think I will. Where are we going?" I asked.

"To Legends. There is a party going down tonight. I can guarantee you the crowd is going to be twenty-five and older."

I looked at Daniels looking like a kid in the candy store. I said, "Okay, I'll go but if anything happens there tonight besides me getting danced on, you owe me a full tank of gas."

Daniels threw his head back in laughter and said, "Okay, I got you."

We talked for a little bit longer, then he exited my office. The rest of my day went by smoothly as I finished up paperwork. Once five-o-clock hit, I sprinted lightly out of the door and to my 2013 Chrysler 200. Connecting my phone to the Bluetooth, I drove the thirty minutes it took for me to get home listening to Sade. My home was my sanctuary, I loved the peaceful quietness of it. When I first decided to buy my home, I thought about staying as close to the *'hood'* as I could.

The *'hood'* was where I grew up and the streets practically raised me. I had spoken to my grandmother one day and she told me that when I chose my house, to not worry about being so close to the *'hood'*. She said, I was going places and I should start living like it.

That's when I found my four-bedroom, two family home in Amsterdam, New York. I had fallen in love with it as I rode past it one day. The outside was painted a crème color and trimmed in black. There was a small garden sitting next to the front porch filled with tulips and roses. There was a 'For-Sale' sign swinging on a post as I walked up the cobblestone walkway to the stairs and onto the porch. The front door was wooden and had an oval shaped window in the middle of the door. I rang the doorbell hoping the person selling the house was there. I got lucky when I heard someone unlocking the door.

"How can I help you?" A little old lady asked opening the door far enough to stick her head out.

Of course, I thought, she thought I was a criminal from the way she was looking. Luckily, for me, I was still in my Army garb and hoped like hell she wasn't a racist.

"Yes, ma'am. I'm sorry to disturb you, but I couldn't help but notice the 'For-Sale' sign. May I look around?" I asked, in my most professional sincerest voice.

She smiled and said, "I would love to show you, but I think it would be better if you come by tomorrow while my son is here. It would just make me feel more comfortable."

"Yes, ma'am I understand. Do you have a number where I can reach you?" I asked.

"Yes, it's five-one-eight, two-three-three— oh look, it's just your luck. My son is pulling in now," she responded looking behind me.

I turned around and saw this tall four-hundred-pound dude walking our way. When he walked up he shook my hand and gave his mother a kiss.

"Richard this young man here wanted to look at the house. Do you mind showing him, while I go and check my roast?"

"Sure, thing Mama," he said.

I introduced myself as we walked inside the house together. The living room was spacious with light brown carpet and decorated with flower couches, a coffee table, a tube T.V., and a cherry wood china cabinet. Next up was the kitchen. It was more updated with all stainless steel appliances. There was an island in the middle of the kitchen with white cabinets and grey marble countertops. The sink was in the middle of the island and pots hung overhead. All the cabinets and countertops matched the island as well. Off in the far-right corner of the room, was a white wooden dining table and matching chairs with grey placemats. We moved on up the stairs it was a single set going straight up and at the top, you could go either left or right. That's where the rooms and bathrooms were.

On the right side, the half bathroom was there, with two massive bedrooms. Both had matching white carpets, red and gold curtains, dressers, tube T.V.s, and matching flower bedding.

We went to the left side; the full bathroom was on that side and was decorated in a light purple and white. The two bedrooms on that side were smaller and looked like those were Richard and his mother's rooms. They had the same matching white carpeting and kind of looked like the other two rooms except for the curtains in one room was pink and white, and the other room had green curtains. The other differences inside these rooms were that one smelled like moth balls and the other smelled like corn chips.

Next up was the backyard. The grass was exceptionally green and mowed to perfection. There was a larger garden in the back which consisted of fresh vegetables. The backyard had to at least been half of a football field. I was in awe. There was an underground pool connected to a Jacuzzi. On the side of the pool where the Jacuzzi was, there was a fireplace made from cobblestone. If I wasn't sure about buying the house before, I definitely was now. I made sure I grabbed any contact info they had because in a few days I wanted to be buying that house.

I took my boots off at the door, sunk my feet into the carpet, and dragged my tired body up the stairs to my bedroom. One of those massive bedrooms served as my room, which was decorated with white walls trimmed in light brown. I had a sixty-inch flat screen T.V. mounted on the wall in front of my king-sized bed. On the right side of my bed was the walk-in closet filled to capacity with clothes, I have been dying to wear. My wardrobe consisted of my uniforms most of the time, so I barely got to wear any of the clothes that were in there.

I walked into the closet and began looking through my clothes. I finally took out a pair of light grey fitted

'True Religion' jeans, a white and grey striped short sleeved shirt, and a pair of all-white hi-top Nike Uptowns. I placed my clothes on the Ottoman and went to go lay down until it was time for me to get ready.

~Erica~

"Girl, I know, you better be ready," I yelled walking into Quinn's bedroom.

Something told me, I should've knocked before I opened her door, but no I wanted to walk right in. Before my eyes was Quinn riding her boy toy, Lavar like the cows was coming home. I covered my eyes, walked out, and waited in the living room. I laughed at the compromising situation as I sat on the couch flipping through the T.V. channels.

When Quinn and I met in Junior High School, I thought she was stuck up. She'd always be to herself and always had a screw face. We became friends because there was this girl in our class who I swear like hell was older than what she was. Her name was Beatrice she was the class bully. She looked like a grown woman and stood taller than everyone in the class, even the boys. She would pick and choose who she'd bully each week. It just so happened she decided to bully me this week. I had a few friends that I hung out with but no one I figured would come to my defense if need be.

This day I came to class and got my things ready for class to start. Beatrice came out of nowhere and knocked all my books off my desk. My mouth hung open as I watched her walk past me laughing. I rolled my eyes and picked my things up but she decided to double back, and smack the back of my neck, hard. She held onto her stomach and laughed a hearty laugh. I closed my eyes trying not to allow the tears to fall, and that's when I heard Quinn.

29

"Beatrice why are you always picking on people. You are too big to be picking on people," she said.

The room got quiet in anticipation of Beatrice's response. Everybody had pretty much gotten used to her being a bully and never thought to stand up to her, including me.

Beatrice walked over to Quinn, got right in her face and said, "Who's going to stop me?"

Quinn was smaller in size and height compared to Beatrice but she puffed out her chest and said, "I will."

"You and what army? I will destroy your little ass."

"That might be true, but everybody is tired of you being a bully. Maybe if somebody would beat your ass then you would stop."

Beatrice screwed up her face and laughed again. She went to walk away, but everybody was shocked when she stopped and backhanded Quinn so hard she flew from her seat. At this point, I was looking on, wondering when the teacher was going to walk in and stop this. Quinn got up with a red hand print on her pretty light skin and stood in Beatrice's face. Her eyes were red, and tears threatened to fall, but she didn't let them.

She began punching Beatrice in the face with a closed fist until she fell to her knees wailing. Quinn didn't stop she kicked Beatrice in her face until the teacher came in and pulled Quinn off Beatrice. Quinn was sent to the principal's office, I was stuck in my seat in shock, and Beatrice went to the nurse's office.

The sound of the door closing snapped me out of my thoughts. I saw Quinn come inside the living room. She was dressed in a robe and had the screw face on.

She said, "What the hell, don't you know how to knock?"

"I wasn't expecting you to have company. Go get in the shower so we can go."

"Don't rush, me."

Quinn left me in the living room as she went to get ready. By ten-thirty we were walking out the door to our cab. The line for Legends was long as hell but thank God I knew the guy throwing the party. We were on the VIP list and it didn't take long to get inside. I told Quinn to order us some drinks while I went to the bathroom. Luckily, for me, I didn't need to wait in line. I went inside one of the stalls, I quickly used it, and made my way back to Quinn.

~Quinn~

For the party to have just started the club was kind of crowded. I ordered Erica and I an Apple Martini and stood at the bar waiting for her. I sat in my seat and danced to the music. I had been sitting there no more than eight minutes when this country bumpkin looking dude came over and asked me for a dance. I happily declined his offer but he didn't walk away without calling me a bunch of stuck up whores and bitches. I simply smiled, threw him my Ms. America wave, and went back to my drink. Finally, Erica came back from the bathroom, threw her drink back, and dragged me onto the dance floor. I would have spilled my drink if I didn't catch my footing.

We tore the dance floor up as usual until they decided to throw on something slow. You know how they throw on those bump and grind songs trying to have one of these dude's dicks hard, but the song be your song so you just two-step to it and turn down every dude's offer. Yeah, that was me pretty much at this point.

As I was slowly rocking my hips to the beat of *'Lotus Flower Bomb'*, the hairs on the back of my neck stood up. I felt someone's presence, but the club was now so crowded, I could barely turn around. I felt this guy's muscular frame and almost didn't want to move. His body moved along with mine and I was shocked. Not too many guys could keep up with me. I smiled as his frame and cologne engulfed me. When the chorus came on he leaned into my ear and sung it, if that didn't almost make me throw my panties at him, I didn't know what would. I had enough of the mysteriousness of this guy, I turned around and couldn't believe I recognized him. His white teeth shined under the strobing lights of the club.

"Well isn't it nice to see you here?" he said into my ear.

I smiled and said, "Likewise."

"Are you here by yourself?"

"No, my friend is with me. Speaking of, I must find her. It was nice seeing you again, Jason, right?" I said, looking into his adorable brown eyes.

"Yes, hold on though, Miss Quinn. I want to get to know you better. Is there any way I can get your number, so I can take you to lunch?" He asked, holding onto my hand.

"I have your number remember?" I responded.

"True, but I have a feeling you won't use it," he said with a chuckle.

There was only a tad bit of truth to his statement. He was interesting to me and I did want to know his story.

"How about this? Let me find my friend to make sure that she's cool, then I'll meet you outside and we can talk for a little bit. I could use the fresh air."

"Sounds good to me," he said kissing my hand.

I smiled and walked away fanning myself. I shook it off and went to find Erica. When I did she was sandwiched between two dudes drinking from a beer bottle. I let her know, I was stepping outside quickly for some air. She gave me the okay signal with her hand and I walked out.

The fresh air welcomed me like a robe and slippers. There were still people waiting on the line to get in. I looked around and found Jason who was standing at the corner talking to someone. I walked over and smiled when he noticed me. I stood off to the side and let him finish talking to his friend.

"Quinn, come here," he said extending his hand towards me.

"Yes," I said looking up at him with my hand inside his.

"This is my buddy, Kareem. Kareem, this is, Quinn. Remember her from Subway earlier?" Jason stated.

"Yes, I do. It's nice to meet you. I'm going to leave you two and go back inside. Hopefully, I can find someone as beautiful as you in there. So, far I've seen nothing but ogres," he said with a chuckle, causing me to chuckle too.

They pounded fists and Jason began walking me around the corner from the club and my hand instantly went inside my purse, where I was able to get a hold of my pepper spray. He stopped walking and looked at me funny.

"I'm not going to hurt you. I just wanted to be able to hear you a little bit better so that we aren't still shouting," he said with his hands up in surrender.

"You can't blame me. I'm a woman and there are some weirdo's out here."

"I'm a soldier. I would never do anything to jeopardize that. You have my word, I am not a creep or a weirdo."

Something told me I could believe what he said, and I eased my hand out of my bag. When I did he smiled. We stood there for the better half of an hour talking and getting to know each other. I found out he had been in the service for nine years. He was an only child to a one parent home. He didn't know his father, and he never asked about him. He was twenty-nine, no kids, and owned his own home. He wanted to have a family one day, and he assured me when that day came he would be there for the child and its mother.

I took all that he said in and began telling him about myself. Of course, I left out the abuse I saw inside my home at a young age. I didn't feel it was appropriate currently. I didn't realize how late it was getting until he had mentioned we were out there for a half an hour. At this point, I didn't want to go back in because of how we were clicking. Instead of staying like my mind was telling me we walked back in and danced the night away. When Legends began to let out, I grabbed Erica and got a cab home.

The next morning, I rolled over right into Erica, whose mouth was hanging open and hot. I squeezed my eyes shut and sat straight up. My head throbbed, as I tried to remember what happened after we left the club. Erica was snoring so loud, I feared she would wake up the neighbors. I giggled to myself, as I dragged myself to the bathroom to do my daily routine of correcting my hygiene. After washing my face, I stared back at myself with a smile on my face.

"Damn, I'm hella fine,' I reminded myself.

Making my way into the kitchen, I got together breakfast for Erica and me. While the bacon sizzled, I checked my phone and noticed Jason had text me. He said, he enjoyed my company last night and he was hoping sometime soon he'd get to take me out. A smile spread across my face as I responded and finished our breakfast.

My mother always used to tell me, that once you were trying to be happy, there was always someone lurking in the background to throw salt in your game. That became a reality when I saw Lavar calling me. I rolled my eyes and reluctantly picked up.

"Hello, Lavar," I said, hoping he detected my attitude.

"Good morning, beautiful. What are you doing up so early in the morning? I figured you would still be sleep."

"If you thought, I would still be sleeping why would you call me?"

"Easy now. You don't have to bite my head off. I just wanted to know if you were doing anything today?"

"Actually, I am, I had a long night, last night and all I want to do is to catch up on my ratchet T.V. and lay in bed."

"Can I come join you?" he asked.

I would have agreed, and usually, I do but I just wanted to be alone and rest off this hangover.

"Not today Lavar, if I feel better later, then sure."

"Okay, I guess I can accept that. Talk to you later."

"Bye."

I hung up and went back to my room to see if Erica had awakened. She was still on her back with her legs spread eagle and her mouth still hanging open. I shook my head and grabbed her purse off the bed and ended up dropping her purse. As I scooped everything up I noticed there was a small plastic baggie. My eyes damn near bugged out of my head, when I noticed what was inside. I was so shocked, I forgot how to be mad for the moment. I walked over to the side of the bed that Erica was sleeping on and shook her.

"Erica—Erica! Wake your ass up we need to talk!" I shouted ready to slap the spit out of her mouth.

MIMI

Chapter Three

I'm beginning to lose sleep
One sheep, Two sheep
Going cuckoo and cocky as Kool Keith
But, I'm actually weirder than you think

~Jason~

Two weeks had passed since I'd heard anything from the beauty from Subway. I'd get a response here and there, but it was never anything to the point, where she gave me real good conversation. I just chalked it up as her not being interested and kept it moving. I didn't know what it was but for the past couple of days, I hadn't been myself. I started forgetting where I was putting things, losing money, and my sleep patterns have been horrible. Making it to work has been nearly impossible for the last week, but I made it. For the first time in a week, I made it to work on time and was surprised there was a bouquet of yellow and white tulips on my desk. I wondered who sent them as I bent down to smell them. I plucked the card from in between the flowers and read it out loud.

'To a handsome guy, I know I've been busy and haven't been able to respond to you, the way we both wanted, but I thought sending you these flowers could be a peace offering. I enjoy the conversations we do have and hope you can accept these tulips as my apology. ~Quinn~'

I chuckled and took my seat, I was getting ready to call her. Until the bathroom door in my office opened and out walked, Quinn. My mind was blown as I watched her glide, yes, I said glide because she didn't walk over towards me. Her hair was straightened, flowing around her face, and down her back. She was wearing a light pink hi-low dress and beige open toe wedges. The only make-up she wore was lip gloss. I thought she looked like a goddess. She smiled and pulled up a chair next to me.

"Surprised to see me?" She asked nudging me with her shoulder.

I chuckled and said, "You can't tell that I am."

"Yes, I can. That's why I asked."

"What made you come and see me?"

"Like I told you in the note, we've been so busy we've barely spoken to each other. I just thought we should change that," she said smiling.

I couldn't help myself, I smiled too. Quinn stood up from her seat and stood in front of me.

"Wait a second. Let me close this door, I don't want any interruptions," I said.

I closed the door, took my seat again, and watched as Quinn came out of her shoes. The smile remained on her face as she leaned in and kissed me on my neck. I'd thought several times about the first time we'd have sex, I didn't picture it in my office. At this point, I didn't care. I'd waited long enough for this moment, I was taking it any way I could get it. Quinn's smooth lips left sticky lip marks on my neck as she began unbuttoning my uniform shirt.

"Have I ever told you, I love a man in a uniform. It turns me on in the worst way," she whispered in my ear.

"No, you never told me, but I would like for you to show me," I said just above a whisper.

The smile appeared on her face again as she continued unbuttoning my shirt. The anticipation was killing me and if it couldn't get any worse, somebody knocked on the door. I cursed under my breath and asked Quinn to give me a moment, while I saw who was at the door. She nod-ded in agreement as I walked away to answer the door. I opened the door just enough to stick my head out. It was Daniels, he was looking at me with a raised eyebrow.

"What?" I asked impatiently, ready to get back to Quinn.

"Umm, are you, okay?" he asked.

I peeked my head back through the door and Quinn was leaning against my desk, winking at me.

I looked back at Daniels and said, "Yeah, I'm kind of busy, though. What's up?"

"I heard you talking to yourself, so I thought, I'd make sure you were alright. I thought maybe you had a phone call. The way the conversation was going I figured you weren't and wanted to check in," he responded. He looked me up and down and tried to look behind me.

In a whisper, I said, "Remember, Quinn, the girl from Subway?"

"Yeah, I remember her?"

"She came to surprise me, I was about to try to get a quickie until you knocked on the door."

"Err Braxton, I didn't hear no female in here with you," he responded.

I looked at him and sucked my teeth. "Of course, you, ain't hear her. I'm not supposed to be in here trying to get a quickie."

"Dude, I didn't hear a female's voice, I only heard you."

I looked at him trying to see if he was lying about not hearing Quinn's voice.

I twisted my lips up and said, "You just trying to peep her to see what she is working with. She still fully dressed, though," I chuckled, opened the door wider and let Daniels in.

He looked around the room, and to my shock when I turned around Quinn was gone and so were the flowers. I rushed over to my office bathroom and looked inside to see if she had run in there to hide from Daniels but she wasn't in there. I stood in the middle of the floor scratching my head trying to figure out where the hell she went. Daniels looked at me like I was crazy and as if he wanted answers.

"Are you sure she was here?" he asked.

"Yes, I'm sure. Why would you think I was lying?"

"Did you get some sleep last night?"

I couldn't lie to Daniels. He knows I haven't been getting any sleep.

I said, "No I didn't. I don't even remember the last time I got some sleep."

"Well, maybe you were just daydreaming. You need to go to the doctor, to see if they can prescribe you a sleeping aid."

"I don't need any medication."

Daniels smirked and said, "Keep on not getting any sleep and you gonna be in here daydreaming about other things. We don't need to walk in here and catch you with your pants down humping the air. I watched as Daniels held his stomach bending over laughing at my life.

"Fuck you, that's not funny."

Daniels made his way to the door and said, "Yeah, yeah. Seriously, though, you need to think about that. I read that not getting enough sleep isn't healthy, it can have you hallucinating and shit. We don't need that around here. By the way, you, remember the eighteen-year-old boy that was here last week asking for information?"

"Yeah, what about him?"

"He's here, I think he's ready to join the Army," Daniels said then saluted me on his way out.

I could hear him cackling all the way down the hallway. I looked around my office again and checked in the bathroom to make sure Quinn really wasn't there. Maybe I should go see the doctor because hallucinating and daydreaming at work isn't good for me. I would hate for what Daniels said to come true. I looked down at my uniform and noticed my pants were unbuttoned and shook it off, while I made my way to the front.

~Erica~

I was dreaming peacefully, laying on the beach in the Cayman Islands. The sun was kissing my milk-chocolate in just the right ways. I had shades on my face and a one-piece, thin, cotton bathing suit on. My feet dug into the sand and my ice-cold slushed Bahama Mama sat next to me. The sound of the ocean waves crashing onto the beach relaxed me, and I felt this was happening. I sat up to take a sip of my drink and wondered where Quinn was. I just knew I couldn't be on this beautiful ass Island by myself. Then I noticed in the distance there was this figure coming my way, calling my name. I recognized the voice as Quinn's.

I smiled because I knew, she wouldn't leave me alone. The closer the figure got to me the farther it got at the same time. Her calling my name was clear though, I stood up to try and make my way to her to close the distance between us. As I began to walk, water came from nowhere and splashed all over my face, causing me to gasp and wake up from dreaming.

"Erica!" Quinn yelled.

I slowly opened my eyes and Quinn was standing over me with a glass in one hand and her hand on her hip with the other. My head spun as I tried to sit up now drenched from the water she threw on my face.

"What is wrong with you throwing water on me? I could have drowned heifer," I calmly said wiping the water from my face.

"You got a lot more to think about if you think drowning is gonna be the death of you!"

"What are you talking about, and why are you yelling?"

I could tell Quinn was furious. Whatever had her panties in a bunch, I knew I had to tread lightly. I watched as Quinn paced back and forth in front of the bed gathering her thoughts. After a few minutes of silence and pacing, she took a seat on the bed and exhaled.

"Erica, I want you to be honest with me," she said in a shaky voice.

"I'm always honest with you girl. What's wrong?" I asked, now becoming scared at what she wanted to know.

Before she responded my eyes swept across the room, I noticed my purse had been dropped on the floor and my heart jumped into my chest.

"Are you doing drugs?" she finally said.

I knew that was coming after I saw my bag on the floor. "What—girl, no. As long as you've known me have I ever done anything besides smoking a little weed here and there?"

"No, you haven't, but why would this be in your bag?" Quinn turned to me holding up the small plastic baggie with white residue stuck inside of the bag.

"Remember the guy that was throwing the party last night?" I asked.

"Yeah what about him?"

"He wanted me to make a sale for him in the female's bathroom, but we ended up leaving before I could," I said. I slapped my hand on my forehead, "Dammit. I'm gonna have to pay him back for that."

"Then why is it empty, Erica?"

I got up from the bed, picked up my purse and looked inside. There was some white stuff at the bottom of my bag. I pinched it between my fingers and said, "It must have fallen into my bag."

Quinn looked at me and I tried to detect if she believed me or not. At this point, I just wanted this heat off me. I knew if she found out I'd been sniffing coke our friendship would be done. Quinn was my best friend, I loved her dearly and I didn't want that to happen. I knew she didn't like to have friends that did drugs since she found out at one point in time her daddy had started sniffing coke. From what little bit she told me, her daddy had lost his business, then he began to spiral downward and took to alcohol and drugs. She didn't want that around her, because she didn't want to have to relive the pain she felt as a little girl.

"Erica, can you promise me something? I know that you may not be doing this but this shit brings back too many memories and if this happens again, just warn me."

"I got you, girl," I said and hugged her.

"Okay, good. Now come on so we can eat this food and watch some ratchet T.V."

I followed her to the kitchen, then it dawned on me. What was she doing in my bag in the first place? I had to ask, "Quinn, quick question."

"What's up?"

"What were you doing in my bag?"

"I wasn't in it intentionally, heifer. I was moving it from off the bed and it dropped. Don't nobody want nothing in your funky bag," she said as we continued into the kitchen to enjoy our breakfast.

MIMI

Chapter Four

How would you feel if she held
You down and raped you?
Tried and tried, but she could
Never escape you

It was going on a month before, Ernest could find it in his heart to tell his wife, Giselle he'd lost his job. No scratch that, he lost his whole company because he was trying to keep it under wraps that he'd been cheating on his wife. In Ernest's mind, it was okay for him to be happily married, with kids and still be able to have his ice-cream on the side. But, where he began to get messy, was when he started having an affair with his secretary, who ended up getting pregnant with his child. This resulted in Ernest telling his mistress she had to terminate the pregnancy.

Esmeralda the mistress, grew infuriated and told him there was no way she was going to kill her unborn child. She slammed the phone down in his ear and thought that would be the end of that. She obviously didn't know the real, Ernest. That same night, he drove over to her house once his family went to sleep. Ernest had been drinking and wasn't in his right mind, but what could he do? How would he look if it got out to his family that he had an affair, and was fathering a child with another woman? It didn't make sense to him, so this trip was necessary.

He climbed out of his car and looked up at the building where Esmerelda was staying. To be just a secretary, she was living in a decent building and he was surprised, she did. He had never been to her house since he didn't want to risk running into someone he knew that lived in her area, so when they would have their affairs they'd drive an hour away from Schenectady.

Ernest was now at her apartment, thinking about how he should approach her door. He was furious and wanted to kick her door down. Even through his clouded mind, he knew it was too late for him to act a fool. He didn't want too much attention drawn to him. He didn't want to risk having to spend the night in jail. Thinking in the right mind, he raised his hand, knocked on the door, and waited until Esmerelda opened it.

Her face read shock when she noticed it was Ernest at her door.

"Ernest, what are you doing here so late?" Esmerelda asked closing her robe tighter around her body.

Ernest couldn't help but stare at her beauty. His wife was amazingly beautiful, but Esmerelda came close. Being from Panama, she had deep brown skin, full lips, slanted dark brown eyes that turned light if the sun hit them in just the right light. She also had thick hair, that flowed down her back, but the difference between his wife and Esmerelda was that Giselle wore her hair in a braid, while Esmerelda preferred her hair out and wild. Her curves were dangerous, and Ernest took it upon himself to take a ride on her.

"May, I come in, Esmerelda?" he asked trying his hardest to contain his anger.

"Sure," was her response as she moved out of his way.

Ernest walked into the dimly lit living room. He looked around and noticed the room nicely decorated. He took a seat on the couch and watched as she walked towards him and took a seat opposite him.

"Why are you doing this to me, Elda? Haven't I taken care of you thus far?" Ernest asked.

Esmerelda exhaled, "Ernest if that's what you want to talk about, you can wait until morning. I've told you

*time and time again, that this is my first child. I will not
kill him or her, because you are trying to protect yourself
from your wife. You knew, what you were doing when you
laid down with me the first time. I told you, I didn't want
this to go any further than a one-night stand."*

*"Bullshit, Elda. You never said any of those things to
me. I cannot allow you to have this baby, Elda. Please
just listen to me."*

*Esmerelda jumped up from her seat and said, "Who
are you fooling? I told you from the beginning, I didn't
want to get serious. You think I didn't know that you had
a wife? I knew the whole time. Remember, I work for you.
I've seen you and her with your children. You wanted to
keep this thing going because you couldn't get your hands
out of the cookie jar! This is your mess and you must live
with it. And might I add, that you sitting here blaming me
for things you say, I didn't say. Why didn't you suggest we
wear condoms often? You knew just like I knew, I wasn't
on any birth control! You have some nerve coming to my
home almost one o' clock in the morning talking about
this! Go home to your wife and children!"*

*Ernest watched Esmerelda pace back and forth in
front of him steaming mad. He grabbed his jacket that
was on the arm of the brown, suede couch and walked
towards the door. Esmerelda followed behind him. Once
at the door, Ernest looked behind him at Esmerelda. Before she knew it, Ernest had her pinned against the wall
by the throat. Her eyes shot open, and she tried to grab
in oxygen to no avail. Ernest was so close to her, she
could now smell the whiskey on his breath.*

*"Listen, if you know what's good for you, you will kill
that bastard. I will never be around. I will make your life
a living hell. I will make sure, you never work a day ever
again. You will have to rely on welfare forever. If you
know what's well, kill that baby," he said menacingly.*

Esmerelda's eyes darted all over the room only wanting to be able to breathe again. Tears slid from her eyes as she prayed silently in her head. When their eyes linked, Ernest smiled and winked at her. He gave her one tighter squeeze, letting her know he meant business. He let her go and watched as she slumped to the ground gasping for air. He walked out of the house thinking that, that would be the last time he saw her. That was just the beginning to his end.

Back to the present day, he sold his business a month ago so that he could pay for Esmerelda to go away. He didn't want to have anything to do with her or the child she carried. All the back and forth to court was putting a dent in his pocket and he didn't want Giselle to start getting suspicious. So, he decided to sell his business to pay her off. Half of a million dollars was worth it, too.

Ernest walked into the house just a little tipsy and noticed his wife had the table set and was placing the food on the table. His children, Quinn and Donald sat at the table like they always did, when they knew he was on his way home from work. His wife smiled, as he entered the kitchen. After washing up for dinner, he sat at the table and enjoyed his meal of broiled steak, roasted potatoes, cauliflower, and an ice-cold beer. Throughout dinner, Ernest tried to decide how he was going to tell his wife what was going on. His mind was so full that after dinner, he just went to take a shower, retreat to their bedroom, and waited for Giselle to come in. The kids were to go to bed right after dinner and a shower, he knew, he had some time before Giselle would settle in for the night. He watched the nightly news to pass time.

"How was your day at work, honey?" Giselle asked coming in dressed in a long silk, pink nightgown. Ernest knew she was hoping to get some sexing tonight just by what she was wearing.

"Same old thing," Ernest said and took a swig of his beer she'd brought him.

Giselle looked at Ernest and knew there was something wrong. She could tell by the lines on his forehead, that it was deep. Usually, she would stay out of his work business, but she was concerned.

She said, "Honey, is everything, alright?"

Ernest sighed and said, "No, it's not."

Giselle sat next to Ernest. "Well, what's wrong?"

"I need to tell you something."

"Okay, I'm listening."

"Well, I sold the business," he said.

He thought, he might as well come with it, so he wouldn't have to beat around the bush. He watched as Giselle rubbed lotion onto her arms and then cleared her throat.

"It's because of that whore, you had sex with, isn't it? The one that you got pregnant?" she asked calmly.

Ernest's eyes opened wide in shock. He didn't know, she knew. "Uh, yeah, but how did you know?" he asked.

"Ernest, a wife knows everything. I'm just surprised, you let her get away with this. As much as you put your hands on me, I figured you would do the same thing to her. How could you be so stupid? How could you do something so drastic?"

"What do you mean, how could I be so stupid?" Ernest said becoming angry.

Giselle jumped from the bed in a huff and folded her arms. "Exactly, what I said! You took food from our kid's mouths, clothes off their backs, and a roof from over their head, all because you wanted to keep a bitch who is having your child silent! How dare you, do something so damn stupid, Ernest?"

"I don't know, who, you think you talking to that way, but you need to watch it. You are lucky I even told your ass about it!"

"How could I be so lucky if I knew it before you told me? I knew about, Esmerelda, way before you even went to her house, to threaten her to get rid of her baby! You are so low down and dirty, that it's a shame. I think you are a lot of things, but this right here takes the cake. How could you take from your kids to keep some random whore silent? But, I knew everything! If you were more of a husband and told me this from the beginning, we could have come up with a plan, and you wouldn't have to sell the business. You are just a dumb, nigga!"

SLAP!

Giselle stumbled backward from the shock of the backhanded smack. There was silence between them, as she held her hand on her face and stared at him.

Ernest eyes were red and bucked from his anger. "I don't give a rat's ass what you think! I am the man of this house, you will talk to me like you got some goddamn sense!"

In a whisper, Giselle said, "Ernest, I'm leaving you. I'm tired of allowing you to put your hands on me. I don't deserve this."

"You will do as I say, and you will take whatever, I do to you. You aren't leaving me!"

"Ernest, this has to stop!" Giselle said and tried to back away from Ernest.

He yanked her by her nightgown causing one of her breasts to pop out. He cocked his hand back and with a closed fist he beat her in the face. She clawed at his eyes trying to get him off her, but it was to no avail. He let her go and she fell to the ground trying to cover her breast that hung out of her nightgown. She laid on the ground whimpering because she felt her eye instantly swelling. Ernest was curing her out something bad and she couldn't do anything but lay there helplessly. Every time he walked passed her, he would kick her in her stomach.

"See, if you, knew what to say out of your mouth, then we wouldn't be going through this," Ernest said kneeling to her face.

She held her hands over her head, so she could possibly block whatever hits he tried to lay on her. Ernest pushed Giselle onto her back and tried to climb on top of her. She knew right then, that would be the chance she got to fight back. They wrestled around on the floor until she kicked him in his nuts and slid from under him. He held his hands between his legs as he went down.

Giselle was stuck at the scene, she finally saw that she'd done something to stop the beatings. She had found an out and with no further hesitation, she turned around and tried to run out of their room. She was on her way to wake her children and tell them they were leaving. She didn't know how much time she had but she was determined, she was going to at least wake them up. She must have moved too slow because before she even made it out of the room. Ernest grabbed her ankle causing her to fall and bang her face on the floor.

"Ernest, please," Giselle whimpered.

"You, really, think you going to leave me? And you got the balls to fight me back," Ernest said and dragged her further into their room.

Ernest once again was able to climb on top of Giselle and for some reason, he was turned on. Giselle fighting back had taken him to a level of ecstasy, he had never reached, and it didn't make it any better that Giselle was practically naked. Ernest began to grope Giselle's breasts causing her to pause in her thrashing to see what he was doing. She put two and two together and began screaming and clawing her way away from him. Ernest finally was able to pin Giselle down on her back and hold her down, by pinning her arms with his knees.

A smile crept onto Ernest's face, as he squeezed and flick Giselle's nipples between his fingers. Giselle begged *for him to stop but that only made his manhood harder and excited him even more. Ernest salivated from the mouth, as he pushed her breasts together and stuck his dick in between and began to pleasure himself. Giselle cried for him to stop.*

"Please, Ernest, I just want to get up and get in the bed. I'm sorry, I won't leave, just please let me get up," Giselle said.

"Shh-shh-shh," Ernest said as he watched the tip of his dick hit her bottom lip.

She tried to turn her head, but he would just smack her face until she surrendered. Ernest got off, Giselle and she rolled over to get up, but Ernest wasn't done with her. He dragged Giselle by the hair and pinned her over the bed. She jerked and moved trying to get him off her.

"No, please don't, Ernest!"

"Yes, Giselle, you need to be punished for talking to me the way that you did. You know better than that." Without warning, Ernest bent his knees, forced himself inside of Giselle, and pumped in and out of her ferociously.

"No, Ernest, it hurts! Please stop!"

"Oh, my goodness! It feels like it has been forever since I dipped into your honeypot. I forgot how good this was. Just stay still, I'll be done before you know it."

Ernest held her down by the shoulders and stood onto his tiptoes to dig inside of her deeper. Giselle couldn't fight anymore. She knew, if she didn't stay still, he would never finish and at this point, all she wanted to do was curl up in a whole and die. She stared off into space as he repeatedly slapped her ass and pulled her hair. She felt him slow down and quickly he entered her anally without any lubrication. As tears fell from her eyes she vowed that the moment she could, she would be leaving him, she knew, he would kill her sooner than later.

"Don't you ever in your life tell me you are going to leave me. You and my kids mean the world to me. I swear if you attempt to leave—I—will—fucking—kill—you—aaahhh," Ernest *yelled, pulled himself from her ass, and jerked himself off until he was drained all over her back and ass.*

"I hate you," Giselle *mumbled under her breath.*

She had never felt like she was scum, but at that moment when she realized, her husband felt it was okay to hold her down and rape her. She couldn't help but feel like she was bottom of the barrel scum. Unbeknownst, to Ernest and Giselle, young Quinn and Donald had stood by their bedroom door listening to the whole thing. Donald vowed, once he was old enough he would punish his father for the heartache, Ernest caused his mother and Quinn hated his guts.

~Quinn~

For the first time in a long time, I was floating on cloud nine. Jason and I had finally decided, we'd go on our first date to this cozy little Jamaican restaurant called Roy's in Albany. While I got ready to go, I shook like a leaf from nerves. It had been a while since I'd been out on a date with someone new. I hoped things wouldn't go bad. Erica had come over to help me, but all she did was lay across my bed and flick through the channels on my T.V.

"I don't know what you're going all out for this dude for. He's just like any ole other guy," she said with her face twisted up.

"He's not just any other guy," I responded while looking over the shirt I had taken out of the closet.

"How do you know he's not like any other guy? This is the first time you are going out with him. You don't know anything about him. What if he's not actually an army dude?"

I giggled. "Erica, you, sound silly. How can someone fake being in the Army?"

"Girl, you, haven't seen those videos on Facebook?"

"Umm, no, I haven't. And right about now, I don't particularly care for them," I expressed.

I was torn between a midriff crop top and a shirt, I could tie into a knot in the front. I walked over to the Bluetooth speaker sitting on the nightstand and lowered the music down. I wasn't up for Erica's mess today.

"Well, I'm going to tell you, anyway. There was this guy who dressed up in an army uniform. Real soldiers dressed in their civilian clothes called him out. He didn't know they were army officials until they asked him his ranking. Girl, he was straight embarrassed. Now, I ask you once again, how you know, he's not faking it?"

I threw the midriff top on my bed, placed my hand firmly on my hip and gawked at Erica. "Girl, you, are working my nerves something bad right about now. Can't you just be happy I have a date tonight, and it looks like this is going somewhere promising."

Erica sat up on my bed. "Sorry, girl, I am happy for you, but nowadays you can't be too cautious. You must remember that people do fake the funk. Remember, when we were younger trying to be hot in the asses and wanted to get with Fredro and his boys?"

I threw my head back and chuckled at the memory. "Girl, we just knew, we were grown and ready to throw our young little pussies on them until they pulled out their shits. Girl, I ain't never been so scared in my life."

"We used to be scared of the dick, now we throw lips to the shits, handle it like some real bitches," Erica howled mimicking *'Lil Kim's Big Momma Thang'*.

"You said those lyrics all wrong," I said holding my stomach laughing.

I'd finally decided on ripped, faded, high wasted *Seven* blue jeans, a simple pink shirt, and pointed toe black five-inch stilettos from DSW. I left my hair wild and curly and put on my diamond stud earrings and silver bangles. To complete my outfit, I rocked my pink and silver shoulder purse.

"Oh, my goodness, you look so pretty," Erica said and touched my hair, that she rarely saw in this current condition.

"Thank you, I hope Jason, thinks the same thing," I said and gave myself the once-over in my full-length mirror.

I turned to look at myself from behind, I was satisfied with the way my butt looked in my jeans.

"Do you really think this is going to go somewhere?"

"I hope so."

"But, you, barely know him."

"That's true but that's why it's called the dating stage. This is where you get to know someone and decide if you want to take it further or not. From what we talked about, he seems like a pretty level-headed guy, and that's what makes him so different than the other guys I've dated."

She didn't think, I noticed, but after I made that statement, she rolled her eyes and went back to flicking through the T.V. channels. Two minutes later, there was a knock on the door and both Erica and I looked at each other. I knew it wasn't Jason because he wanted to meet at the restaurant. Erica shrugged her shoulder's and we both walked to the door.

"Who is it?" I called out.

There was silence on the other side, until I heard, "Uh, it's Jason."

A smile crept across my face as I unlocked the locks on my door and opened it. Jason was on the other end of the door holding pink and white roses in a glass vase. He passed me the flowers, and I, in turn, passed them to

Erica. I gave Jason the once over and gave his outfit a mental check mark. He was wearing a plaid blue and white button-up shirt, black slacks, and black square-toed shoes. His hair was freshly cut, and his teeth were shining brightly.

"You look amazing," Jason said.

"Thank you. You don't look too bad yourself. What are you doing here? I thought, we said, we would meet at the restaurant?"

"I know, but, I decided to surprise you and come pick you up. I'm sorry for just popping up. I hope you don't mind, I did a little background check to get your address," Jason said.

"Um, no, I am really surprised, though."

Jason's eyes wandered my body from head to toe and his smile spread more. "Are you ready to go?" he asked.

"I sure am," I responded with a smile of my own.

I noticed his eyes were now focused on something behind me, I realized that fast, I had forgotten Erica was there. I turned, and she was standing there with this goofy smile on her face.

"Aren't you going to formally introduce us?" Erica asked.

I may have been tripping but her voice was oozing with sexual lust.

"Oh, yeah, where are my manners? Jason, this is my best friend, Erica, Erica, this is Jason," I said.

Erica reached her hand out and Jason shook it. "It's nice to meet you," he said.

"Likewise," Erica said looking him up and down.

She lingered on his crotch and I almost smacked her eyes out of her head.

"Come on let's go," I said pushing Erica out of the way giving her the eye.

She looked down cause she knew, I was going to get in her ass once I got back. Jason grabbed ahold of my hand and we walked out of my building. In front of my building, there sat his car. I was shocked to see that he was pushing such a nice car. I tried to hide the excitement behind a smile. He opened the door for me and waited until I had my seatbelt fastened before he closed the door. The seats inside his car was so soft, I felt like I melted right into them. Jason climbed into the car, turn the radio to a jazz station and drove off.

We made small talk for the better part of the drive. He was funny and very smart. I didn't fall shy of being smart and our conversation was very intellectual. We talked about everything from the weather to sports and politics. Throughout dinner, Jason kept a smile on my face and laughter rolling off my tongue. Time slipped by so fast, I didn't realize until it was time for the bill to be paid. I had a few dollars on me, but I knew the bill was way more then what I had in my pocket. Without hesitation, Jason grabbed the bill, placed his American Express Black card in the billfold and waited for the waiter to come back and collect. I was impressed he didn't ask us to go Dutch. But, as bad as I had begun to dig him, Dutch would have turned into ditch real fast.

"Do you have any other plans for the rest of the night?" Jason asked looking down at his watch.

I looked at my cell phone to see that it was only reaching eleven o' clock and I didn't have anything planned. "No, I don't. Do you have something in mind?" I said.

"I actually do. I was wondering if you'd like to accompany me back to my house for a glass of wine, maybe?"

A smile spread across my face. "Sure, I'd love to," I responded.

The waiter came back with his card and as he placed a twenty-dollar tip on the table, we gathered our things and left. The ride to his house was quiet besides the sounds of 'The Quiet Storm' playing on his satellite radio.

57

What shocked me the entire ride, was that he held my hand. I prayed this thing, whatever it was I was feeling, would progress into something beautiful. We reached his house in Amsterdam and I was amazed at how big it was. He escorted me from the car and into his house. I would be damned if I wasn't in shock. Everything was beautiful from the fabric on the couches to the paint on the walls.

He tugged on my hand and led me through the living room, into the kitchen, and out to the back door. Lights in the ground lit up as we walked down a cobblestone path, to what appeared to be a shed. This is where my heart dropped to my ass. I thought I was about to see my last moments getting chopped up. To my surprise, when he opened the doors, he clicked a light switch and the space brightened up.

"This is my relaxing place," Jason said and walked inside.

Inside of the shed like space was a bookshelf lined with books, framed pictures of what I assumed to be his loved ones, two light brown couches, and carpet on the floor. There were glass end tables beside each couch and a glass coffee table. A T.V. sat in the far-right corner along with two game systems and a rack with different games and movies. In the far-right corner was a bunch of pillows that looked like they were as soft as clouds.

"This is beautiful." Those were the only words I could get out, as I walked up to the wall that hoarded the most pictures.

I looked at each one. Some of them Jason was in and others were just of the same people.

"If you don't mind, I'm going to run into the house and grab the wine and some glasses."

"I don't mind."

"Make yourself at home." Jason smiled, then turned and jogged back to the house.

I took this time to check my phone, the only person that had tried to contact me was, Erica. She texted me back to back asking me what time I was coming home. I rolled my eyes, powered my cell phone down, and made my way to look at his selection of books. I was amazed at how many self-help books he had. He had a few urban fiction novels, but the self-help books overpowered them. Jason came back as I was placing a book back onto the shelf.

"I didn't know if you preferred white or red wine, so I brought white. Is that cool?" He asked shining his bright teeth.

"Yes, it's fine," I said and took a seat on one of the couches.

Jason poured us both a cup and sat down next to me. "So, tell me some things about you. You were kind of quiet during dinner."

"I really hate to admit it, but I was nervous," I said with a chuckle. I was still nervous, but I wasn't about to let him know that. I continued, "Somethings about me, hmm, it depends on what you want to know."

"Well, I'd like to know, why is it that you aren't snatched up in a relationship. I'm pretty sure a beautiful queen such as yourself would be with someone."

"It's been a while since I've been in a relationship. The reason is that my last relationship didn't go too well. Who am I kidding, it was horrible. But, I think that conversation should be discussed later," I responded remembering my last relationship.

I didn't have any trust in the relationship and it had turned me off so bad, I decided not to commit to anyone until I could trust again. That was how I only kept Lavar as a friend with benefits. I looked around the room and at the ceiling of the shed. The top of it had been replaced with glass and I was amazed to see a few stars in the sky.

"Are you open to being in a relationship?"

I thought about my answer before I responded. Was I really open to a relationship? I know, I was hoping that what I was experiencing with Jason would go somewhere, but what woman wouldn't think that way after such a great night.

"I am open to a relationship. However, I must be able to put my trust into the person, I am with. I gained some major trust issues from my last relationship and I wouldn't want to carry those issues over into something new. You know?"

"Yes, I totally understand. That's why you see so many self-help books up on that shelf," he said with a chuckle.

"What happened in your last relationship that made you realize, you needed to turn to self-help books to get you through?"

Jason took a sip from his glass and exhaled. He leaned back on the couch and looked at me in my eyes. "I was engaged to be married and I was at the alter when I found out she decided to leave me for my cousin. Then I found out she had been cheating with him the whole time we were together. Said she was pregnant with my baby and it turned out that it wasn't mine."

My eyes almost popped out of their sockets. I couldn't believe what he was telling me. "I'm sorry to hear that. Women can be so damn trifling. They do things like this and then they complain that there aren't any good men around. Some of these women irk me," I said.

Jason chuckled again and said, "I understand where you're coming from. You, know what, I came to grips with it, and I've moved on from it."

I placed my cup on the coffee table in front of me and turned to Jason. I made intense eye contact with him. "When things like this happen to a man, do you guys feel the same way women do when they lose the love of their life?" I asked.

"I can't speak for all men, but, I can completely see how women feel when men do the things they do. I was heartbroken and at my worst, after this happened, but I couldn't do anything to change it. I took it as a sign from God letting me know 'Listen, Jason. I gave you so many signs and you ignored them, but I'm going to give you this sign, right here to show you, bruh, this girl isn't for you.' And you know what, I was glad I wasn't one of those dumb dudes who would see the signs and still go through with the marriage."

"I'm glad you weren't the type to still go through with it," I said taking a long sip from my cup.

Jason licked his lips and eyed me. I felt his eyes on the side of my face when he said, "Oh, yeah, why is that?"

"You think if you would have stayed with ole girl, you would be sitting here next to me?" I asked flirtatiously.

"Touché."

~Jason~

The sunlight shined so brightly it hurt to open my eyes. My head pounded, as I placed my hand over my face to block the sun from burning a damn hole in my face. It took me a little while to realize I was in my relaxing spot. The previous night's events came back to me slowly, then I realized there was dead weight on my arm. Quinn was sleeping peacefully next to me and I smiled. She was laid on her stomach and her hair was crowned around her face. I brushed the hair from her face as I remembered that it got heated last night.

She kicked my ass in 2K15. After the ass kicking she laid on me, we switched from wine to Henny, then after that, I don't remember anything else. I'm pretty sure we didn't have sex because we were both fully dressed, minus our shoes. My eyes couldn't help but ogle over her body and I couldn't help but appreciate it.

"Shit, I got to get up," I said out loud to myself.

My arm had fallen asleep and was beginning to tingle. I didn't want to wake her though, because she looked like she was enjoying her sleep.

"Daddy, no, leave mommy alone. Momma!" She yelled in her sleep, stunning me. She jumped and woke up breathing hard.

"Are you okay, Quinn?" I asked not sure what the hell just went on.

Quinn hurriedly sat up and grabbed her head. "Oh, God, this headache. Yes, I'm fine, sorry," she said.

I sat up and dropped one leg over the couch so that she was now sitting in between my legs. I rubbed her back and smiled to let her know she was good.

"Would you like some aspirin and orange juice?" I asked.

"Please, this sun is something serious. Maybe you should have thought about transforming the roof."

I chuckled. "Oh, no, I got that covered," I said.

I walked over to the wall, where the light switch was, there was a button I could press. I gave it one push and motorized blinds began to move across the glass ceiling, then the sun slowly faded. I watched as she laughed and fell on the back of the couch. I told her, I would be back with her things and left. While I was in the house, I checked my messages and decided to give Kareem a quick call.

"What's up, partner?" he answered groggily.

"Man, you still sleep?" I asked cheering hard as hell.

I wanted to let him know about my night with, Quinn but I didn't want to take too long.

"Yeah, fool, it's ten o' clock on a Saturday."

"Get your ass up and get ready. Let's go play some ball in like two hours."

"Seriously, Jay, man."

"It's a tradition, I'll call you when I'm on my way."

I hung up and made my way back to the shed. Quinn had laid down on the couch and looked like she'd fallen asleep again. I placed the orange juice and aspirin on the table and turned on the T.V. to see if I could catch a bit of news.

"Thank you," Quinn said moving to grab the juice and aspirin.

"Anytime, beautiful. Sorry, I got you drunk last night," I said chuckling.

"Oh, my God, it's a little foggy, but I enjoyed myself. It's been a while since I've thoroughly enjoyed myself."

"Man, you kicked my ass in 2K last night."

She laughed and covered her face. I couldn't help but think that her laugh was gorgeous.

"I couldn't help myself, 2K and Call of Duty are my joints," she said.

"You want to play a quick game?" I asked challenging her.

"Not with this headache. Oh, shoot, what time is it?"

"It's just after ten, you ready to go already?" I asked taking a seat closer to her.

She looked me up and down and I'll be damned she bit her bottom lip before she turned her head away. I won't lie, my homie down below sprung to life and I crossed my legs to hide it.

Quinn looked at me again. "I'm only ready if you have something to do," she said.

The lump that formed in my throat was a mixture of lust and because I didn't know how to take her response. She could have meant *'bend me over and take me, right now'* or *'we can chill for a while longer until I decide I'm ready to go.'* I didn't know how to take it. I wanted to be truthful with her and let her know what I was feeling. Then at the same time, I didn't want to give her a chance to shoot me down. I'd have my tail between my legs for sure.

"Can I be honest with you?" I asked finally getting that knot from my throat.

"I would like for you to always be honest with me."

I scooted closer to her and said, "We are both grown, right? I don't know if you feel it as well, but I think there's something going on between us. We have a natural connection with each other like we've known each other for years. I mean, I know it's still kind of early and we still have a long way, before we could ever say, this is my man, or this is my woman. And God knows that one day, I would love to say that. But—"

"Anything after but is bullshit. And I'm going to stop you, right there. Don't get me wrong, Jason, I like you and I would like to take whatever it is that we have to the next level. I just don't know, what kind of girl's you are used to dating and I'm up on game. I'm not the type to give it up after the first date," she expressed and proceeded to gather her things.

I stood there in shock watching her gather her things. I finally snapped out of it after a few seconds. "What? No, that's not where I was going with that, Quinn. I respect the fact that you don't give it up after the first date. Not too many girls can say that. I was just going to say, I hope you'll be open to going out again sometime soon."

She turned towards me with an apologetic smile and embarrassment written all over her face. "I feel like complete shit for that, I apologize," she said.

I walked towards her with a smile on my face and grabbed her in my arms. She laid her head on my chest and my lips connected with her forehead.

"I accept your apology. Just know that my goal isn't to just smash and send you on your way. I do see myself with you. You are smart, beautiful, and you have a personality out of this world," I clarified.

"Thank you," she said blushing.

"Come on, I'll drive you home," I said.

She put her shoes on her feet bending at the waist. My eyebrows and my manhood raised up. I shook my head and grabbed her hand as we walked out.

'It would have been nice to lick the clit, though.' I thought and laughed to myself. We climbed into my car and I made my way back to Schenectady, hoping I'd get the chance to see her again.

~Erica~

My phone was vibrating somewhere on the bed and just waking up and trying to find it was giving me a headache. The night before, I got silly drunk and this hangover was something major. I felt around the bed for my phone and instead of finding the phone, my hand caressed another person's leg. I jumped up, pulled the covers back, and was shocked to see who was in Quinn's bed with me. I began to shake him to wake him up as I looked at the display screen on my cell phone. When he woke up I told him, he had to go, and it needed to be fast. I picked up the phone call before it went to voicemail.

"Hello," I said.

"Are you still at my house?" Quinn said.

"Yeah, I'm still here, are you on your way home?" I asked moving around the room quickly, throwing his things at him.

"I am already back in Schenectady. We stopped at Burger King to get something to eat. I should be there in like ten minutes."

"Alright, yes, I'm still at your house. You know I hate going home with all those people in my crib."

"Well, that's why you need your own spot. There ain't nothing like coming home to peace and quiet," Quinn giggled.

"Who you telling? I slept so good last night in your big ass bed."

"I bet you did. You better not have had one of your little flings in my bed again."

"Girl, please."

Her tone became serious as she said, "Girl, please my ass. That's disrespectful as shit, Erica. I would never do no shit like that to you."

"Oh, my God, Quinn. That was like two years ago. Get over it, I didn't have nobody over here."

"Alright, whatever you say. I got to go, Jason, is back."

I scrunched my face up and said, "You can't talk to me while you around him or something?"

"Erica, I'll see you, when I get home," she said and hung up.

I threw my phone down onto the bed and walked to the door.

Levar looked at me and smiled. "Girl, if I knew, you did the things that you do, I would have been gotten up with you," he said.

"Listen here, dude. Last night was a mistake and it will never happen again. I don't even remember what happened last night. And if Quinn finds out, that's my ass and yours. Right about now, I'm not in the business of losing her as a friend."

"Well, then you shouldn't have called me last night, begging me to come dick you down," he bragged.

"Brag all you want but remember, I just said, I don't even remember last night," I repeated with a smirk.

"You are such a bitch."

"Your mama's a bitch. Now get out before Quinn come home."

"Whatever tell my boo, I'll hit her up soon."

"Boy, if you only knew, she wasn't thinking about you," I said nastily to his back.

I closed the door behind him and rushed back to the room. I had to get the funk of sex out of her room and change her sheets before she walked through that door. I was just fixing the pillows when she walked in. She had this goofy ass grin on her face when she threw herself onto her bed. I couldn't do anything but stand there with my hands on my hips.

"What?" she asked still with that stupid smirk on her face.

"Hello to you, too. You just walked in here and didn't say anything and then you didn't even bring me something to eat."

Quinn sat up in her bed. "Girl, if you don't cut it out. There is food in here and I didn't buy this."

"I hope this new dude don't have you acting brand new like Lavar did when y'all first started talking," I mumbled taking a seat on her bed to put my shoes on.

"What is your problem?" she asked.

"Ain't nothing, I'm going home, I'll hit you up later," I said. I didn't understand why I was in my feelings about her going out with Jason, but I was. Ever since me and Quinn had been friends, she was never serious with a guy. Hell, the way she came in the house smiling like the cat from *'Alice In Wonderland'*, she'd never done with another man.

"Erica, what is wrong with you?" Quinn called to my back as I made my way to the door.

I turned around and smiled. "Nothing, I'll call you later, and maybe we can get something to drink. Cool?"

Quinn raised her eyebrow. "Cool," she said.

No more words were spoken as I headed out the door. The wheels in my head turned, as I thought about why I was so mad. I should be happy, that she was happy, but I just couldn't find a happy bone in my body. In my eyes, I figured, Quinn out of all people should be able to find the guy of their dreams and grow old being happy. After all that she had dealt with growing up with, she deserved it. So why did I feel this way? Why did I feel like my best friend was being taken away from me and they'd just started to begin to date?

Before entering my building, I signaled for one of the dope boys to meet me in my building. Once inside I copped me a thirty-dollar bag of some sticky and went into the house. I couldn't wait to strip out of these clothes to get my high on. As I cracked open the plastic baggie, I took a deep breath and inhaled the potent aroma. A smile crept across my face as I expertly began to roll it up in a White Owl Cigar.

Chapter Five

I'm friends with the monsters
That's under my bed
Get along with the voices inside of my head

~Jason~

The lights overhead was so bright, I had to squint my eyes to scan the room. There were advertisement posters to get tested for STDs and HIV on full display. I usually, wouldn't take anyone's advice about going to the doctor, but Kareem was serious about me seeing one. He thinks I need a powerful sleeping aide to get my mind back on track. I laughed and said that I was fine, but it didn't stop me from waltzing inside of the doctor's office. I exhaled, as I focused on the clock on the far-right wall, watching the seconds tick by. It had been ten minutes since the nurse left and it seemed like it took forever for the doctor to call me back.

"Mr. Braxton, I haven't seen you in a while. What brings you in today?" Doctor Clark spoke looking into my files.

"I've been having trouble sleeping and I've been doing my fair share of daydreaming. My buddy Kareem thinks I should get something to help me sleep," I spoke.

"Hmm, well, from your chart it looks like your vitals are good. What kind of trouble are you having? Are you not sleeping at all?"

"I am not, in two nights I'd say, I'm not even averaging a full six hours."

"I'd like to run some tests and send you to a neurologist."

"Okay."

"In the meantime, I'll prescribe you Restoril. It's going to help you fall asleep and keep you sleep. Take it about thirty minutes before you climb into bed," Doctor Clark stated, writing out the prescription.

He handed it to me as well as a referral to see a neurologist. He gave me a handshake and I was ready to leave when there was a knock on the door. I turned around and noticed it was Doctor Clark peeking his head in. I looked at him confused and wondered if there was anything else he was forgetting. Doctor Clark came in the room with a look of confusion on his face.

"Is there something you are forgetting?" I asked.

"What do you mean, Mr. Braxton? We didn't have a chance to begin." Doctor Clark said looking over the chart he had in his hand.

'What in the hell is going on?' I thought.

I slowly took a seat in the chair and answered his questions. Once he was done he asked me why I was ready to go if he didn't begin the initial questioning for the visit. I explained to Doctor Clark what had just happened. It caused him to slightly look at me in shock. I wasn't completely sure what had just happened, but Doctor Clark sent me on my way with a prescription for Ambien and a referral to see a neurologist for the following week. By the day, I felt like I was becoming less and less of myself.

~Quinn~

It had been a full two weeks since I'd heard anything from Jason. He claimed he saw something promising happening between us and then just fell off the face of the earth. For days I waited for him to call me, to ask me out on a second date, but the call never came. The truth of the matter and something I would have to face is the fact, he just probably wasn't that into me. My days waiting for his calls had been filled with Erica and I lounging around my house doing nothing. Finally, on the fourteenth day, I just said forget him and decided I'd move on to the next one. This was one of the main reasons why I wouldn't allow myself to get attached to someone. As soon as I thought it would work out, I face planted right into the ground.

Erica and I decided we'd head out for some drinks and maybe go shake a tail feather or two. At around seven o'clock Erica and I began getting ready to go to a club called the RBC Jazz Club out in Troy. It took me almost an hour to figure out what I wanted to wear. Finally, I decided on turquoise, black, and white printed Steve Madden tights, a white crop top that showed off my cute belly, and on my feet, I decided to wear black open toe sandals with tassels. I wore my hair curly and placed silver chandelier earrings in my ears. While I had gotten dressed Erica was in the bathroom doing her thing. A quarter to eleven, my cell phone rang. There was an unknown number flashing across the screen and I hesitated to answer.

"Hello," I answered.

There was hesitation from the other party before I heard, "Come open your door."

"Who is this?" I said. '*Who the hell is this playing on my phone and at my door?*' I thought.

"It's me, can you open the door?" the voice asked.

He sounded like his best friend died, I knew who it was being able to catch his voice. I pressed the end button and made my way to the front door, as Erica was coming out of the bathroom. She asked what I was doing, and I placed my finger in the air telling her to hold on. I cautiously unlocked the door and on the other end with his head down was Jason. He slowly looked up at me and flashed his smile. He brought his arm to extend between us, he held a white lily bouquet. I smiled and grabbed them.

"Oh, I'm sorry. I didn't know, you were on your way out. I should have called before being an ass and just coming."

"Oh, no, you're okay," I said happy inside that he had made his way to come see me.

"I'll just come back tomorrow."

Erica crept up behind me and said, "Are you almost ready?"

Jason smiled politely. "Hello, Erica, sorry to interrupt you guys. I just wanted to see your face, Quinn. Go and have a good time," he said.

I peeked over my shoulder, Erica was eyeing Jason until I nudged her to take her ass back to the room. Once she got the hint, she slowly dragged her ass back to the room. I turned my attention back to Jason.

"Actually, I'm, glad you came by," I said.

"Really?" he said widening his eyes.

"Yes, um, would you like to come in?" I asked.

The smile and wink he gave told me he didn't mind. I placed the lilies inside of a crystal vase and sat them on the center of the coffee table. Jason got comfortable as I excused myself to go and speak with Erica. As bad as I wanted to go out and have a few drinks with her. I had been waiting two weeks to spend time with that man in the living room. Erica would either just understand and still go or be mad and either way, still leave. I walked into my room and Erica was sitting on my bed with her legs crossed and her arms folded across her chest.

"Don't tell me, you are about to blow off a night out with your friend for some nigga who dropped you like a bad habit?" Erica said with fire dancing in her eyes.

I sighed, "Erica, he didn't drop me like a bad habit. If he did, he wouldn't be here, right now."

"But you haven't heard from him. This nigga can just waltz back in your life, then you just drop everything for this nigga. A nigga you don't even know,' Erica said loudly.

"Erica, please don't be mad," I said.

A few moments passed as Erica stared at me like a hawk. A smile spread came across her face. "You know what, Quinn? I tripped just a tad bit because for the last two weeks I watched you watching your phone, waiting on this nigga to call. Him showing his face tonight is something that neither you nor I could control. I apologize, enjoy yourself."

I was taken aback by her sudden mood change. "Are you sure?" I asked.

"Yes, girl, I'll just go by the bar have a drink and then bring my ass back home," she said reaching in to hug me.

I reciprocated hesitantly. "Call me and let me know you got in," I responded.

"You got it. Well, let me get my fine chocolate ass down to this bar," Erica said with a wiggle in her hips and the smile plastered on her face.

"Chocolate is cheap baby girl, you're fudge," I said to her.

She paused in her step as she turned around and looked at me. For a quick second, her smile turned into sadness. There was even a little mist in her eyes. But two seconds later, the smile returned, and she began to walk away again.

"I'll call you."

"On your way out, let Jason know, I'll be there in a few minutes, I have to use the bathroom."

"A'ight, shorty," Erica said.

She made her way to the door as I made mine to the bathroom.

MIMI

Chapter Six

You missed a spot - there
Baby would you mind tasting me
It's making me all juicy

~Jason~

"Sorry for taking so long. Would you like something to drink?" Quinn asked me as she dried her hands against the tights that she wore.

My eyes roamed from her feet, up her legs, lingering on her bare stomach, and finally to her face. I smiled and grabbed her hand.

She walked in front of me and I said, "No, thank you. I just want you to sit right here and listen to me." Her face scrunched up, I knew she wanted to know what I needed to say.

"Okay, I must prepare myself. Let me go pour me a drink," she said.

I chuckled as she scurried out of the room. I clasped my hands in front of me as I put my head down. My palms were sweaty, and my heart raced. I looked up at just the right moment, and Quinn's hips swayed right in front of me, as she took the seat next to me.

"You, good now?" I asked leaning back into the couch and stretching my legs out in front of me.

She giggled and said, "Yes, I'm good."

I cleared my throat. "I want to apologize for the absence. I had to get a few things in order, that needed my focus."

"I understand, I'd rather you take care of the things you needed to handle before you come back this way. I just figured that a simple phone call would have been appropriate."

"You are right about that. I had no time to do so with all of these appointments I had."

"Appointments?" she questioned.

"Well, yes, I had to go see a neurologist, but things are okay," I said looking at her with the same confused look, she was giving me.

Her mouth dropped, and I instantly knew what she was thinking. I couldn't help but laugh which caused her face to turn red.

"Oh, my God, I feel so embarrassed," she said.

"For what?" I asked through my laughter.

If looks could kill, Quinn's side-eye glance would have killed me dead. I checked my laugher and waited for her to speak.

"I feel so silly admitting this, but, I thought you had a little girlfriend you had to break up with," she admitted.

"Baby girl, you think, I would have invited you back over to my spot if I had somebody else?"

"I don't know, y'all men are slick," she said waving her hand at me.

A smile spread across my face and I moved closer to her on the couch. I used my index finger to guide her face in my direction.

"Listen to me, there isn't another female in the picture. I'm not that kind of guy. I will keep it one hundred with you like no other. I will have you wondering where I've been all your life. You will forget all those lames you fucked with in the past," I assured her.

Quinn's eyes darted around me fast as she tried to figure out where she wanted them to rest. I felt her breath blowing on my lip as her eyes finally landed on my lips. I could tell her heart was racing as I drew closer, only centimeters from her face. Moving my hand to the back of her neck, I pulled her in for our first kiss. Her eyes shut instantly as well as mines did. We had the same desire to savor this kiss. Her mouth opened to receive my tongue in her mouth.

As passion took over and the next thing I knew, Quinn was laying under me with her legs wrapped around my waist. I was trying my hardest to keep my manhood from rising between her legs. Quinn's hands rubbed up and down my back until she grabbed the hem of my shirt and reached under to touch my bare skin. My fingers were tangled in her hair as I softly nibbled on her neck. She let soft moans escape from her mouth as my tongue went further down into her shirt. My hand slipped under as I took her breast into my hand and squeezed.

I looked at Quinn whose eyes were closed, and her head was tossed back. Her pelvis thrust upwards into me. My mouth replaced her bra, swallowing her nipple and areola into my mouth. I withdrew her breast from my mouth and flicked my tongue over her nipple.

"Oh, my God," Quinn moaned.

My tongue circled around her nipple as my free hand slowly began to make its way down her stomach. I pulled the elastic band from her body, my hand traveled into her leggings and rested over her lace panties. Quinn's body got stiff under me causing me to pause and not go any further. I looked up at her wondering why she'd stopped.

"Is everything, okay, you want me to stop?" I asked slowly moving my hand away from her soaking panties.

"I just want to make sure this, what we have, is what you want? I want to know this isn't going to be a hit it and quit it type of thing," she said as she looked at me.

At that moment, I knew, Quinn was used to getting hurt. I looked into her eyes and vowed that I would be the one to save her from that.

"I can assure you, Quinn Elise, this is what I want. What we have happened fast. But, this by far is the best, I have felt about anything in my life."

"Then, no, I don't want you to stop," she said just above a whisper.

I bit my bottom lip and sat right up on my knees. I pulled her leggings and panties off catching a whiff of her scent. I winked at her and said, "Open up for, daddy."

Chapter Seven

Three Months Later

Cause after we kissed
I could only think about your lips
Yes, I remember boy
The moment I knew you were the one
I could spend my life with

~Erica~

My plane landed back home at exactly 7:25 p.m., Quinn had insisted on meeting me there, since I'd been gone for almost a week. Thanks to my new boo. He'd requested we go on a four-day trip out to Florida to his parent's estate. When he presented this idea, I was initially shocked and didn't want to go. That was until he told me, his parents were going out of town and wanted him to house sit. Who was I to pass up this offer? Even though my boo and I had only been together for three months, I felt complete. I thought about him as the plane pulled up to the gate and began to unload passengers. A smile crept on my face because I knew deep down inside he was the one for me.

I came out of my daze, grabbed my *Puma* duffel bag, and walked off the plane. The duffel bag was the only bag, I'd taken with me resulting in my bypassing of the baggage claim. I walked right out of the Albany airport and looked around for Quinn.

'*She told me, she would be here,*' I thought.

I did one more sweep of the cars lined out front of the passenger pick up. I noticed an all-black and chrome '*2013 Range Rover*' with tinted windows pull up. The driver's side opened and out walked, Quinn. She was dressed in faded blue jeans, a peach H&M V-neck, a white leather jacket, and white six-inch pumps. Her hair was in a bun and she had pearls in her ears. Her shades covered her eyes and her makeup was laid to perfection. I pulled my shades down the bridge of my nose until it was at the tip and eyed her up and down.

"Well, look at you, looking like a bag of money," I said.

Quinn giggled. "Well, you, know how I do," she said.

"Whose whip is that you are pushing?" I asked.

She gave me a look that said, I should have known better asking that question. "Girl don't try it, Jason, recently bought that truck," she responded.

"And he letting you push it already?"

We made it to the truck and I couldn't help but peek. The seats were leather, and the dash was made from black wood grain and chrome. I placed my bag inside the trunk and climbed inside. The truck still had that new car scent and everything.

Quinn started the car and said, "Am, I not his woman, why not?"

"I just figured, he'd want to play with it a little bit longer."

Quinn eased into traffic and we headed out to Schenectady. I was glad I was home but sad I had to leave my boo. Things were still fresh, and the honeymooning stage was perfect. The sex was out of this world. I felt my panties getting moist just thinking about how the four days we were gone, he tore into this kitty in every single way.

"Erica," I heard Quinn calling my name.

"Huh?" I asked coming back from my daze.

"I asked you if you were hungry?"

"No, I'm not, I just want to get home to get some rest."

Quinn smirked and said, "Your boo must have laid that thang on you while you were gone."

"Girl, you don't even know the half of it. My kitty still sore."

"Ewww, that's too much for my ears," Quinn said with a giggle. "When am I going to get to meet him? I've barely heard anything about him, then out of nowhere he's shipping you off to Florida and taking you to dinners," she continued.

I smiled and said, "You know, I don't do the whole thing with relationships. I don't want to jinx this because I think this may be going somewhere."

"That is not fair. You got to meet, Jason, the first day I met him."

I laughed. "Well, duh, I was with you silly. In all seriousness, I just want to take my time with this. Just to see if this is something serious, and not just some wham bam thank you ma'am kind of thing," I stated.

Quinn sucked her teeth. "Girl, he took you to his family's house in, Florida. Although, you, didn't meet his parents yet, doesn't mean he don't take you seriously."

Quinn may have been right, but I still wanted to wait for her to meet him. For the rest of the ride to my house, we rode in silence. My mind was wrapped up in my new boo and I couldn't help the constant smile that was on display. Maybe one day, I could find it in me to introduce Quinn to him. Quinn put the car in park once we arrived and I exhaled.

"What are you doing later on?" Quinn asked taking the time to check her phone.

"Nothing, unpacking probably."

Quinn's loud shriek scared the mess out of me, I turned to stare at her like she was crazy. She was banging on the steering wheel, acting like a complete fool.

"Oh, my God," she yelled.

"Jason is coming back today from his trip to, Texas," she yelled.

"He was in Texas?" I asked.

"Yeah, he had to go down there with some of his battle buddies to help with a grand opening for a recruitment center. He just texted and told me he'd be home later this evening."

"Well, I guess whatever plans you had for us later are canceled?" I moped.

"Girl don't be like that, I'm sure you understand now that you finally got a man."

My mouth dropped open as I burned a hole on the side of her head. I placed my shades on and grabbed the handle on the door.

"Fuck, you, trifling heifer. I'll hit you up tomorrow so that we can get something to eat," I said.

"That's if I come up for air," she replied with the biggest smile I'd ever seen her make.

I rolled my eyes upward as she danced in her seat. I was happy for her, but at the same time why did I feel so salty? I grabbed my bag from her trunk and made my way to my apartment. She honked the horn as she pulled away from the curb. *'I need a damn drink,'* I thought, as I threw my hand up and watched until she turned the corner and disappeared.

Chapter Eight

Tonight, we're gonna do something different,
Tonight, we're gonna touch a little different.
I'm gonna wait on you hand and foot
Like the king you are baby,
Just lay back and I'll show you the way.

~Quinn~

Without another thought on my mind, after I dropped Erica off at her apartment. I looked at the time and realized I had four hours before Jason would be home. I rushed over to *'Price Chopper Supermarket'* to grab a nice, thick, juicy steak, potatoes, and some asparagus, then headed to his house in Amsterdam. Yes, it had been only three months since we'd made things official, but he decided to give me the key to his place, so I could come and go as freely as I wanted to. He said, things had become so perfect for us in the short amount of time, that he felt, I needed the key, and he was right. Sure, things moved fast, but when you developed feelings as fast as we did, why wait?

After leaving *'Price Chopper'*, I made a mad dash to my apartment, to grab some things I thought would be essential for tonight. I was about to show him how much I missed him. My heart was pounding in my chest, as the anticipation got the best of me. It had been a few days since I last seen him, but I missed him like crazy. By the time, I reached Jason's house, the clouds had gotten dark and sparks of lightning lit up the sky.

'A storm wasn't in the forecast today.' I thought as I grabbed the bags from the truck.

Once, I was safely inside, I immediately seasoned the steak and cut up the potatoes to go with the steak. Once, I had the food inside the oven, I checked to see how much time I had left. I had just a little under two hours left before my baby would be walking through that door. I laid out my outfit, which was a pink and black corset, black crotchless thongs, fishnet knee-high stockings that hooked to a garter, and black six-inch pumps. I raced to take a shower and ran around the house like a chicken with my head chopped off looking for some candles.

Twenty minutes before the food was expected to be done, my cell phone rang. I answered out of breath, it was my baby calling.

"Hello," I said.

"Hey, baby," he said.

"Hi, I miss you," I stated, as I took the steak out of the oven and began sautéing the asparagus.

"I know, baby, and I miss you as well. I just got out of the terminal, I'm waiting for Kareem to pick me up. I should be there shortly."

"Okay, baby, no rush."

"Are you at my house?" he asked.

"Yes, I am, I have a surprise waiting when you get here."

I heard the smile in his voice when he said, "Oh, yeah, well let me call Kareem to see where he's at, so I can hurry home."

I giggled and said, "Sure, baby go ahead."

"See you soon."

I hung up the phone and began setting the table. I made his plate, sat it at the head of the table, then set mine next to his. The minutes ticked by, as I waited for him, and hoped I wouldn't have to put the food in the microwave. Twenty minutes later, I heard a car pull into the driveway, and I took my place. One of my juicy ass cheeks sat on the table as I stared at the entrance of the dining room.

"Quinn, where you at?" he yelled from the foyer.

I heard the *plop* of his bag hitting the floor and it felt like my heart was beating out of my chest.

"I'm in the dining room," I called back.

I heard his footsteps coming in my direction and a smile long as the Mississippi River spread across my face. Jason got to the dining room and stopped.

He bit his bottom lip and a grin spread across his face. "Well, damn, if I knew this is what I was coming home to, I would have come home sooner," he said.

"Come have a seat? I just wanted to show you, that I missed you," I said.

I sashayed my way over to him and wrapped my arms around his neck. His arms instantly wrapped around my waist and he grabbed a handful of my butt. I giggled as our lips touched and his tongue invaded my mouth. I could tell he'd had something to drink because I tasted it on his tongue. I pulled away from him and grabbed his hand to sit.

"Baby, with the way you're dressed, and walking around here teasing me. I don't even think, I want to eat," he said, as he rubbed his hand across the zipper of his jeans.

I brushed the hair from my face and smiled. We took our seats and began eating. I honestly wanted to rush through dinner so that we could get to the good part. We made small talk as I asked him about his trip. He asked me what I did while he was gone. Once we were done, I placed the dishes in the dishwasher and escorted Jason upstairs to the bathroom. The candles I'd found was placed around the bathroom, and a tub full of hot water awaited him.

I winked my eye and planted another kiss on his lips. I began to undress him. Then told him to get inside and I would be back to check on him in ten minutes. The bedroom was still in need of my attention, I had to complete it. The California king bed was made with fresh sheets, and candles adorned the Victorian style dresser and the nightstands. As promised, in ten minutes I went back into the bathroom, Jason was relaxing with his feet up and his eyes closed. He looked peaceful and I didn't want to disturb him.

"What did you say?" he asked almost scaring me out of my skin.

"I didn't say anything, baby. I was just admiring you. Are you ready?"

"Girl, I been ready," he said and began to get out of the tub.

As he stood on the bath rug I dried him off with the towel. His dick was already hard and waiting in anticipation. Jason took me in his arms, kissed my forehead, then lifted me up. My legs instantly wrapped around his waist as he walked us into the bedroom. Jason laid me down on the bed and stood back as he admired my body. He took my shoes off and held my legs in the air, as he took in all my shaved glory. He bent my legs and placed my feet onto the bed, then Jason got down on his knees and rubbed his index and middle fingers across my pussy.

I arched my back and thrust my hips forward as his face came closer. His tongue lapped away at my clit causing me to drip with sticky goodness. Jason's fingers expertly penetrated me, and his tongue circled my clit.

"Oh, God," I called out as I felt an orgasm building up.

I didn't want to tap out so soon, but I knew, I couldn't hold it any longer. The speed of his tongue gradually went faster, and I had no choice, but to mush his face into my love box. He didn't stop either, he kept going as I leaked all over his face.

"I hope you not done yet, I'm just getting started," Jason said as he stood up and snatched my fishnet knee highs off my legs.

In one swift movement, my panties came off next. Jason grabbed me by my legs, turned me over onto my stomach and rubbed and squeezed my ass cheeks. Occasionally, he dipped his finger inside of me to make sure, I was still wet. He untied the corset, helped me out of it and demanded I place three pillows under me and bend my knees. I threw my hair over my shoulder and obeyed his command. Jason positioned himself behind me and placed the tip of his dick inside of me.

I gasped as his thickness glided in and out of me. He held onto my waist and dug in deeper. My eyes rolled to the back of my head and my moans escalated. Having sex with Jason was always amazing and just three minutes in, I was ready to cum all over his dick. His fingers interlocked with my hair as he pulled it.

"You love this dick?" Jason asked.

"Yes, I do," I moaned.

"Whose pussy is this?" he grunted.

"Jason—ssss—it's yours, all yours!" I yelled cumming all over his dick.

Jason slowed down and looked at the cum that was on his dick. "Damn, you, missed your man that much?" he asked.

"Yes, I did," I moaned and reached my hand between my legs to tease my clit.

"Turn onto your back," Jason commanded.

I did as I was told and turned over onto my back. Jason spread my legs with his as he intensely stared into my eyes. Jason used one hand to guide himself into me. Even though his love strokes had just left my body, I gasped again as he entered. My pussy muscles tighten around him, as he maneuvered in and out of me. We still held our intense stare as his fingers interlocked with mine.

Moments later, he broke it and buried his head in between my shoulder and my neck.

"Quinn, I've never felt this way so fast for somebody," he admitted.

My nails dug into his skin as he long stroked me. All I could get out was, "I haven't either."

"Do you love me?"

"Yes," I moaned.

"I love you, too."

"Mmmm—harder," I moaned.

He did what I asked as he lifted his body off me and dug into me harder. My mouth dropped as I thrust my hips into him to match his pace.

"Marry me, Quinn. I know it's all too early, but I just feel it in me that you are the one. Just say yes and we can take as long as you want to plan the wedding. Tell me yes, baby."

'Is he just saying this because the sex is amazing, right now? Or does he feel this way?' I thought.

I went back in forth in my mind whether I should say yes or not. Hell, for crying out loud, we'd just told each other we loved each other. His strokes became faster and it slipped out.

"Yes, Jason, I will marry you," I shrieked.

He stopped mid-stroke and looked down at me. The seconds that passed felt like they were minutes. A smile crossed his face and he took my tongue into his mouth. He began to stroke me again and faster.

"Yes, baby, you've made me the happiest man alive." He said with each pump.

Jason wrapped his hand around my neck and applied pressure. My eyes rolled back into my head, as I felt nothing but pleasure. Jason begged me to cum with him and I was almost there. He bit into my shoulder and from the depths of his gut, he grunted, as I felt his dick contract and his seed entered my body. My legs shook as he bucked inside of me. When it was all said and done, Jason laid his body on mine and just stayed there. We were both out of breath, as we slowly fell asleep.

~Jason~

"Braxton, can I see you in my office for a moment." My commanding officer said distracting me from my thoughts.

I had been at work for all of six minutes and was getting ready to start my work for the day. I got sidetracked and thought about the day I asked Quinn to marry me. That was over three weeks ago. When I told Kareem, he told me that, I was out of my mind and I should have waited, but I always went by the here and now. What if we weren't together in the next six months? Why not seize the moment for what it was? Hell, all that mattered was that I was happy and so was she. Tonight, I was going to ask Quinn to lose her apartment and move in with me asap.

"Yes sir," I responded and followed him to his office.

Pierce waited until I was inside the office to close the door behind us. Thoughts juggled around inside of my head wondering what this was about. There were several papers spread out across his desk, as he invited me to take a seat in one of the available chairs.

"I know, you are wondering why you are in my office. I can assure you, I didn't want to bring you in here for this. I know that a few months ago you went to go see a neurologist. I requested for the paperwork to be forwarded to me. At that time, the neurologist said all tests came back clear. There was nothing for you to worry about and that you just needed the Ambien to get you through some sleeping issues you were having. Yesterday your neurologist contacted me and said that he checked again and there was something he missed. Has he contacted you?" Pierce spoke shuffling the papers around his desk.

"Yes, sir. He left me a voicemail on my phone yesterday. I plan on giving him a callback today," I responded with a questioning look on my face.

Pierce folded his hands together as if he was in deep thought. He placed his hands under his chin and began to speak. "Braxton, before I tell you, what I need to tell you, I will call up your neurologist and he can explain to you what is wrong. Is that okay, with you?"

'Hell, no it's not, okay,' I thought.

Shit, Pierce already knew something I didn't, and I wasn't comfortable speaking with my doctor in front of him. "Do I have a choice, sir?" I asked.

"Actually, you do. You can call him on my office phone and I can step out. Give you a few minutes to speak with him."

"Isn't there some kind of breach that the doctor has committed between a patient and a physician?" I asked.

"Being that I am your commanding officer if there is something found that could put you or another at risk of danger. I have the right to know."

'At risk of danger?' I questioned in my mind.

I exhaled deeply and decided on letting Jamison stay. Hell, he already knew what the doctor was going to say. I fumed on the inside, but I sat as cool as a cucumber on the outside. Jamison dialed the neurologist number on speaker and waited for him to pick up.

"Doctor Clark," he said into the phone.

"Doctor Clark, this is Commander Sergeant Pierce. I have you on speaker and Specialist Braxton is here as well."

Doctor Clark cleared his throat and paper shuffled around in his background. "Good morning, fellas, Mr. Braxton, I know that a few weeks ago you came in for a scan of your brain and I told you everything came back clear. I regret to inform you, that once I looked back over the paperwork, your brain activity showed that you are having the beginning stages of schizophrenia. I would like for you to come in for another scan, so I can be sure of this so that we can get you on the right medications."

Doctor Clark continued to talk but I checked out and my mind went elsewhere. Did I hear him right? How can I be schizophrenic? I was at a loss for words and the only thing I could remember was Pierce telling me to go to see Doctor Clark that same day. Also, that, I would be suspended for two weeks until I got the results back. My mind swam with questions as I climbed into my car. I drove away from the recruitment center and found myself at one of my favorite bars.

I played with the thought of entering. Fifteen minutes later, I finally found myself on my way home with a bottle of Crown Royal. My plan was to drown in the bottom of this bottle and deal with Doctor Clark another day.

MIMI

Chapter Nine

Don't know the facts but I saw the blood pour from her head
See I laid down beside her in the hospital bed

All was quiet in the Boyd household. Summertime had quickly approached. Me and Donald had planned to build a makeshift tree house in the backyard. Daddy was stuck in a rut since he couldn't find a job after he sold his business. Mommy tried her best to help look for a job for daddy, but it didn't work in her favor. Daddy told her to let him be a man and to worry about keeping the house cleaned, keeping him and his kids fed and keeping his pussy on ice for whenever he wanted to dip in it. His words, not mine. For me, the household was too quiet, and I didn't like it. The day that everything came crashing down, came soon.

I should have known something bad was going to happen. The weather took a change for the worst. For days the sun shined brightly. I had even gotten a tan behind the nice sunshine. But, this day, it was pouring rain. It was so bad, you could barely see through the rain. Daddy was in the basement all day watching T.V. and Mommy had been cooking and cleaning as usual. When Daddy was in the basement, Donald and I knew not to bother him. It only meant, his face was at the end of some cheap liquor bottle. When dinnertime came, Mommy called Daddy up from the basement.

As Donald and I sat at the table with our heads down, he staggered in from the basement. The liquor he was drinking oozed from his pores and funked up the room. Once my father took his seat, Mom started saying grace and took her seat. The table was quiet all except the sounds of our forks hitting our plates. I peeked at my mother, and from the expression on her face, I could tell she wanted to speak but was afraid too.

"Momma, these potatoes are really good. Did you do something different to them?" I asked.

My mother stopped eating and smiled. "Quinn, yes, I did. I added some cheese to them. I'm surprised you noticed because it wasn't much," she replied.

Donald jumped in and said, "These are really good, mom."

A wide smile spread across her face, I knew my mother was feeling good. We rarely commented on her cooking and I felt she needed to hear something good. I looked over at my father before I began to eat again, he had the nerve to have his face screwed up. I cleared my throat and put my head back down to finish eating. Not even a full minute passed when I heard a smack. My head snapped up and my mother was holding her face with her mouth open. Me and Donald were shocked as well. This was the first time, Daddy had put his hands on my mother in front of us. Sure, we knew what was going on behind closed doors, but Ernest never did it in front of us.

"Damn it, Giselle! Who told your dumb ass to go and change things?" Daddy yelled in her face.

Still holding her cheek, she said, "Ernest, honey, I just thought it would be okay to try a new recipe. It's no harm."

"No harm! What do you mean no harm? You know, damn well, I don't like you changing things."

"But, you, wouldn't have even known if I hadn't said so. I really don't see a big issue, Ernest," my mother said just above a whisper.

Daddy picked up his plate and I thought he was going to dump it. The next thing he did shocked me in all my *fourteen-year-old glory. Daddy grabbed mommy by her long hair and raised his hand to smash the plate in her face. It happened so fast all I could do was sit there and watch in shock. The plate broke against mom's face and blood was everywhere. Her nose was busted and there were cuts all over her face. She howled in pain trying to stop the blood from gushing from her nose and a cut that was under her eye. Mommy fell from her seat, Daddy climbed over her and began raining blows to her body. I saw Donald trying to pull Daddy off Mom. Our father stopped focusing on Mommy and pushed Donald off him, who was punching and pushing him off our mother.*

"Oh, you, think you tough, now? I've been waiting for your little black ass to jump bad! You think you tough, huh, nigga?" Daddy yelled as he stood straight up and stalked over Donald.

Mommy was beaten and bloodied but managed to lift her head from the ground. "Ernest, please, leave him alone. He's just a child," she whined.

"Child my ass. This little nigga here is sixteen, now. He thinks he can go toe to toe with me! Oh yeah, come on big man!"

"Keep your hands off of my, momma!" Donald yelled.

The next events followed felt like they happened in slow motion. Donald put his hands in front of his face and jabbed at Daddy twice. Surprisingly both hits landed and immediately caused Daddy's eye to swell. He was shocked that his own son had hit him. He stood there for a minute touching his eye and looking at his hand. I had moved from my position at the table to help mom up off the floor. She was able to sit up then we saw that Daddy and Donald were, having an all-out brawl in the middle of the kitchen. Donald was picking up anything in his line of vision and breaking it over our father's back. Momma managed to jump up and jumped onto Daddy's back racking her nails against his eyes.

"Get off him, Ernest. You're going to kill him!" she yelled.

I stood off to the side in shock. My heart was pounding in my chest because I didn't know what to do. The hot tears that ran down my face matched the hot urine that slid from my body. I was scared. I watched on as my dad stopped his assault on Donald and flung mommy from his back. She hit the floor with a thud and banged her head against the corner of the stove. The room became still and we all looked on as blood gushed from her head.

"Mommy!" Donald and I screamed.

Daddy rushed over to check her pulse and cradle her head in his lap. "Don't just stand there, go dial nine-one-one!" he yelled frantically.

This was the first time, I'd ever seen Daddy shed tears. The look in his eyes told us that he was scared. Donald dashed into the living room to pick up the phone and dialed 911. My legs felt like jelly under me as I walked over and lowered myself to my knees.

"Is she okay?" I managed to ask.

"Yes, baby girl, she'll be okay. Dammit, Giselle get up," he cried.

He rocked back and forth holding his shirt against the back of her head. Donald had come back into the kitchen with a scowl on his face. Donald took this time to sock Daddy right in the face causing blood to gush from Daddy's nose.

"Donald, stop, don't you see that mommy is, hurt?" I yelled.

"If it wasn't for this piece of shit, nigga, she married. We wouldn't be in this situation. Fuck that, nigga!" Donald yelled pacing back and forth by the kitchen doorway.

I looked at Daddy who was holding the bridge of his nose trying to stop the blood from pouring.

I walked over to Donald and hugged him. "What did nine-one-one say?" I asked.

"They be here shortly, and to not let this sack of shit leave."

"Are they going to arrest him?" I asked lifting my head from his chest flabbergasted.

"What do you think?"

"But, he is our father. Why would you tell them to arrest him?"

Donald dragged me away from the kitchen so, Daddy wouldn't hear us talking. *"I told them because, I'm tired of his shit, Quinn. Look at momma in there. Do you know how long this has been going on? Do you want him to continue and possibly kill her? She dies what happens to us? We shipped off to somebody group home never to see each other again. You think I want that to happen, Quinn, huh?"* he said.

The tears started up again as we paused to listen to the police sirens that were approaching. My heartbeat was so fast I thought that at my young age, I would have a heart attack. Within minutes there was banging on the door and a deep baritone voice yelled for the door to be opened or they were going to kick it in. Donald told me to go sit in the living room. He said he'd come get me when it was time to ride with momma to the hospital. As much as I tried to, I drowned out all the chaos around me, until I heard Donald tell me that it was time to go. Momma was on a stretcher but was conscious and I saw the police taking Daddy away in handcuffs. All the neighbors were in their yards looking on and whispering.

At the hospital, the doctors rushed momma upstairs into the neuro-care unit. They proceeded to examine her to see the extents of her injuries as we waited inside of the waiting room. A nurse sitting at the nurse's station walked over to Donald and I and sat next to me. Donald's face was hard as stone as he looked off into the distance. Not even paying attention to the nurse that sat right next to me.

"Hi sweetie, my name is, Nurse Eva," she said with a warm smile on her face.

I turned my attention to her and grabbed a hold of Donald's hand. I didn't know this lady from a can of paint and knew that this lady had the power to separate my brother and me if something happened to our mother.

"Hi, I'm Quinn and this is my brother, Donald," I said.

Donald eyed me like I did something wrong. "Quinn, keep your mouth shut," he said.

Nurse Eva looked at Donald and I and smiled sweetly, yet again. "I'm not here to harm you guys. I just wanted to know if there's someone you can call to come get you while your mother is in surgery?" she asked.

"Yeah, I'll go call them now," Donald answered.

In the back of my mind, I didn't know what Donald was talking about. Nurse Eva walked away, Donald grabbed my hand and walked us over to the pay phones. I was scared, I didn't know what would happen between my parents. Daddy was already on his way to jail and only God knew how mommy was doing. My head began to hurt as I waited for Donald to call whoever he was calling. The fight between my parents replayed in my mind and the tears fell again.

"We'll be leaving in about a half hour. I called Brian's mother to come get us. They are going to bring us back home and wait until we hear something about mama. Everything is going to be okay, sissy," Donald expressed as he rubbed his hand up and down my arm.

I nodded because all I thought about at that moment was going home and getting some sleep. This was by far the worse fight they had ever been in, and I only hoped we would be able to recover from this.

~Late Night Special~

After hours drinks with my boys was my favorite past time. Friday's are my best day out of the week, for a few reasons. It was the end of the work week and I had my weekends to myself. I could have a couple after hour drinks with my boys, and it was payday.

Kareem and I decided to go to Seth's Pub on State Street to grab a drink and unwind. The week had been hectic since we found out that one of our battle buddies had gotten killed during a tour in Iraq. The funeral was slowly appropriating and we both needed these drinks to prepare ourselves to attend the funeral the following week. I decided to drive my car to the pub so that when I was good and ready to go, I could just leave. Two drinks and maybe even a beer was my limit. I didn't want to be drunk while driving. Seth's Pub had become my favorite spot to relax after I had met Quinn, and just like any other time I came, my favorite bartender, Alicia had a nice cold beer sitting on a napkin in my favorite spot.

"Thank you, Alicia," I said with a smile.

"No problem, sugar. Kareem told me about the week you guys had. I knew you would need it," Alicia responded wiping down the bar top.

"Speaking of, where is he?" I asked.

"Bathroom, he should be back any second."

Just as Alicia said that Kareem walked from the bathroom and joined me for a drink. For four hours we talked trash and laughed doing anything to get our minds off our loss. Kareem was good and drunk and feeling himself buying out the bar. While I took my last sip from my second beer, I told Alicia to make sure he took a cab home and to hold his keys. I received a text from my lady telling me to come home. The text that came was one I'd been waiting for since I clocked out. I patted his back and dapped Kareem in a half hug then proceeded to my car. I looked at my watch and realized that it was nearing ten-o-clock. I slid into the driver seat to take this drive.

***

My car idled as I sat in the driveway looking up at the one-story red brick house. The white shutters on the window were closed tightly, and the light in the foyer shined brightly through the oval-shaped glass on the cherry wood door. I turned off the ignition and walked up the cobblestone walkway to the porch. I placed the key into the lock and took my boots off as I entered the house. All the lights were off except one that was dimly lit inside of the dining room. As I walked inside, a smile spread across my face. On top of the glass table, there was a silver platter and my feast. I walked to the head of the table and looked at the wonderful sight that sat before me. I loved nights like this.

"Well, are you hungry or not?" Erica asked.

I unbuttoned my shirt and sat in the seat. Erica was on top of the platter dressed in nothing but whip cream on her breasts with cherries on top and whip cream covering her pussy. Her chocolate skin was a sight to see with nothing but whip cream on it. I sat in the chair and pulled it closer to the table. She spread her legs wider and I pulled her closer to me, then licked the whipped cream just enough for her to feel my tongue glide over her clit. Soft moans escaped her lips as I pushed my face further into her love box. My tongue expertly slid up and down her clit as my index and middle finger slowly pleasured her. As she thrust her hips in the air, against my mouth. I knew she was ready to cum all over my face.

I abruptly stopped. "Come, show daddy, you missed him," I demanded.

Without hesitation, Erica climbed off the table and got on her knees between my legs. She unfastened my belt and pants and dug around for my prized possession. A smile crept onto her face before she slithered her long tongue out of her mouth and circled it around the head. Her tight warm mouth made its way over my head and down my shaft, causing me to throw my head back in ecstasy. I felt her throat muscles relax as every inch of me slid to the back of her throat and her lips touched the base of my dick. The tip of her tongue tickled the hair on my balls as she bobbed her head up and down. My toes curled while I grabbed the back of her head and kneaded my fingers through her Brazilian virgin hair.

"Yes, make this dick cum," I groaned watching her watch me.

She winked to let me know, that was her plan. I felt myself getting there and at the last minute, I changed my mind and took my dick out of her mouth. She stared at me with a questioning look but knew not to question me. I climbed out of the rest of my clothes and grabbed her by the hand. As we stood behind the Italian leather couch, I bent her over by the waist. She knew what time it was, Erica snatched a condom that was laying close by. I secured it on my manhood and spread her ass cheeks. Spit dropped from my mouth, down her crack, and onto her asshole.

"You want this ass, daddy," she purred.

I didn't think it was possible, but, my dick got harder. I groaned out my response and licked my fingers to lubricate my dick. My head broke through and almost instantly I wanted to cum. I kept my composure and continued to slide in her tight ass. I grabbed her waist, looked down, and watched as my dick slid in and out of her. Her moans escalated as I pumped in and out of her faster. I grabbed a hold of her hair as she screamed out for me to give it to her harder. Moments later, I took my dick out and snatched the condom off.

Erica slid off the couch and onto her knees in front of me, while I jerked my dick off and came all over her face. Her tongue snaked out as she lapped up what cum she could from her face and used her index finger to wipe the rest off and place it into her mouth. The night didn't end there, and I ended up staying there longer then I had anticipated. In fact, I didn't realize how late it was until the sun began to come over the horizon and realized that I had to get in the shower and get home to my fiancée.

~Sleeping Alone~

The morning sun shined through the open curtains in my bedroom, causing me to stir from my sleep. No matter how many times I told myself to never leave the curtains open at night, I still managed to leave them open. Which resulted in the sun shining brightly on my face. I really must start closing these damn curtains. My pink silk Victoria's Secret nightie clung to my body as I switched positions to drape my arm around my husband, but to my surprise, he wasn't there.

Yet, again, it was Saturday and he was off from his job at the recruitment center, but I didn't recall him coming home last night. He didn't call, text, or send me a telegram letting me know he was going to be out.

'I guess I should be used to this,' I thought.

As of late, he had been spending more nights away from home and when I would ask where he was, he'd brush me off. Then tell me to stay in a woman's place and let him be a man.

I sat up in my king-sized canopy bed and looked around the room that I shared with my husband. Everything was in its place and nothing strayed around. Above the fireplace he requested to have built in our room was a recent photo of us together, enjoying a night out on the town. I smiled at the thought of that day. The backdrop was Forty Second, Street. We had gone to see a *'Madea'* play at Madison Square Gardens and a bite to eat afterward. Although he had already proposed to me while giving me the best dick ever, he did it right there in front of all of New York to see.

The smiles that were displayed on our faces spoke so many volumes of true happiness that I wouldn't have thought, I would ever see the day that my fiancée would be spending consecutive nights out. A tear slid down my face, I quickly wiped it away and climbed out of my bed.

"Time for me to get my day started," I said.

After I'd taken care of my hygiene, I made my way to the kitchen to make breakfast, that I knew I'd be eating alone. I also knew that the food would soon get cold waiting for Jason to waltz in. The small television that sat on the marble countertop displayed the news channel. I could only shake my head at the many deaths that had happened within the last week. As I laid down some bacon in the cast iron skillet, I heard the faint sound of the alarm chirping, singling that Jason had made his way home.

'Just in time for breakfast,' I thought.

I listened closely as his keys dropped onto the coffee table in the living room, and his footsteps echoed down the hallway to the kitchen. Jason stepped behind me and placed his lips on the back of my neck, causing my body to stiffen up as if rigor mortis was setting in.

"Good morning my beautiful, Quinn," he spoke.

He grabbed a mug from the cupboard and poured him a cup of coffee that had been freshly brewed. Then he took a slice of toast off the platter that sat next to the stove and took his usual seat at the head of the table.

"Good morning, dear," I responded trying to relax some.

I couldn't help but wonder why after work and a full night out, did he smell like soap.

MIMI

Chapter Ten

*Cause if I let him do it, I did it to myself
And I was so dumb I need it, I need some help!
Cause all that I can see is that she is prettier than me
Damn, I wish I had her body! I can hear my self-esteem
I don't like me!*

The hardest thing I always face with romps with my boo is letting him leave. I knew what I was in for when we started fucking a few months ago. Right, before he proposed to her. For God's sake, he's an engaged man now, so I knew there would never be more. A girl could only hope one day, he'd walk in and tell me he was leaving her for me. Yeah, right, in what crazy world does that happen? So, I settle on being his second fiddle and doing the things for him, Quinn doesn't do. I watched as he got dressed to leave. I sat up in the bed and wondered what it would be like to be his Mrs. What I was doing was fucked up, yes. Although, Quinn has been my best friend for years and always came to my aid when I needed her, I just couldn't shake the feelings I had for Jason.

Growing up in a household where you're constantly getting picked on by your mother is enough to drive anyone crazy. I was almost there, too, after all the times she'd told me, I'd never amount to anything because my skin was so dark. I'd never be anyone's CEO because if I wasn't giving up the pussy, I would never be equal to a lighter woman. The poison she fed me, would forever be embedded in my brain, this is what I'd always lived by. Sure, enough on the outside, I hid the fact that I was insecure, especially when I was standing next to Quinn.

Yes, I am, admitting that I'm envious of Quinn. It all began after her brother went to jail. She was now sad and alone because her mother was gone, and both her father and brother were in jail. I was the only person she had left, so me being me, I figured I would take her out for some ice-cream. Ice-cream makes everyone happy. Although she didn't want to go, I stole my mother's car and went to pick her up. The ride to Bumpy's was a silent one. I felt bad for her and didn't want to ruin anything by blabbing my mouth about something she didn't particularly care for.

When we arrived, I ordered our favorite sundae to share, strawberry shortcake with strawberry syrup, cherries, hot fudge, and lots of sprinkles. I grabbed two spoons, a ton of napkins and made my way to the picnic table where she sat moping.

"I got our favorite," I said almost in a whisper.

For the first time since I picked her up, she lifted her head and smiled just a tad to show her appreciation.

"Thank you, Erica, I appreciate this." A lone tear escaped from her eyes.

I reached over and caressed her hand. "I am your best friend. It's what I'm supposed to do to make sure you're, okay."

"Thank you, you don't know how much this means to me. I've been in my feelings for so long and you've been by my side all this time. I seriously don't know what I am going to do."

"We'll get through it," I spoke with confidence.

At that moment, two college men came up to us and stared Quinn down. My attention adverted to Quinn who wasn't even paying attention.

"Hello," the taller of the two spoke.

I was unsure if he was speaking in general or to one of us specifically, so as Quinn looked up from the sundae, I decided to speak for the both of us.

"Hello."

Quickly glancing at me, he turned his attention back to Quinn and retorted, "I wasn't talking to you tar baby. I was talking to this honey, right here."

Quinn's mouth dropped, flabbergasted at what this dude said. I took his insult with a grain of salt. I'd been called worse and by my mother no less.

"Excuse, you?" that was Quinn.

"It ain't nothing, Quinn. Let's just finish this sundae," I interrupted before this rude fuck boy had a chance to say anything.

"No, I want to know clearly what he said," Quinn huffed folding her arms.

The shorter of the two shook his head because he knew exactly where this was going. Before it got out of hand, he started to grab his friend to drag him away, but his friend insisted on staying and talking to Quinn.

"I was talking to my beautiful, Queen. Blackie didn't have to speak on your behalf," he chimed with a chuckle.

My eyes turned into slits as I looked at him. I'm pretty sure at this point, if looks could kill, his friend would have had to dial nine-one-one. I hated that people thought, I wasn't beautiful just because my skin was darker than most. I looked on between Quinn and this dude, and even though she was defending me, I still couldn't help but feel jealous. They chose the pretty light-skinned girl over the dark-skinned one. That night, even though, Quinn apologized to me for his actions, I still somehow managed to feel like I was dirt at the bottom of someone's shoe.

'That's the thanks I get, for wanting to make her feel good about her shitty family. I should have just left her for dead.'

Jason grabbing his keys from the table brought me back to reality. I sat up against my pillows and reached for my candy, I bought the night before. I opened the clear package, dug my pinky nail in, and brought it to my nose.

Inhaling, the powder went flying through my nostrils, and down to my throat, causing a numbing sensation.

"You, know, I really hate when you leave. I don't understand what you see in her, that you don't see in me," I spoke.

I knew not to say that, but I still did. I truly wanted an answer, but I knew, I would never get one.

"Then stop letting me come over and fuck you any kind of way. You need to stop doing that shit."

I crawled to the foot of the bed and sat up with my legs under my body. I pulled at his pants leg and smiled at him. "You know, you like it when I do all the freaky shit, you want me to do. Is that the reason why you fuck with me?"

"I am not going through this with you, right now. I've stayed long enough."

"When are you going to tell, Quinn?"

"What do you mean tell, Quinn. What? That I am fucking her best friend every chance I get? I'm not going to tell her, cause I don't plan on leaving her. And I for damn sure, don't plan on having her leave me."

I sighed and mentioned, "No, not that, I'm talking about you being medically discharged from the Army."

"I'm not, I'll call you." Without another word, Jason flew out of my house. The one he helped pay for when we first started fucking around.

He said that he didn't want to have to keep coming to the apartment I was sharing with three other people. He said that someone was bound to put two and two together, and they would or could tell Quinn. That was a chance he didn't want to take. Once, he was gone, I walked to the bathroom naked to take a shower. I found a new soap online, I'd been dying to use. It lightened my skin in a matter of days.

~Quinn~

My mind wandered as I watched Jason eat his breakfast. Maybe I was thinking way too much into things. There would be a possibility that there was a bathroom at work that he could have used to take a shower. After all, he had been there all night, and I couldn't blame him for wanting to take a shower. The thought I had of him cheating slipped to the back of my mind. Planning my wedding was now the top priority on my mind. I couldn't stop the smile forming on my face.

"What you over there smiling about?" Jason asked, looking up from his eggs and bacon.

I stood from my seat, walked over to Jason, and stood behind him, massaging his shoulder. "I couldn't help but imagine what our wedding would be like. I have been waiting for this day since I was a little girl."

"Yeah, about that I don't want an outrageous wedding. I was thinking we could go down to City Hall and just throw a dinner party as our reception."

"Really, Jason, this is going to be my one and only wedding."

"I just don't want to spend an arm and a leg on one day."

"One day that will give us a lifetime of great memories."

"I get that, believe me, but babe come on, you've got to be realistic. We can do that at the dinner slash reception."

"But, I just want to have a special day. That means—"

Jason slapped his hands against the table, interrupting my words. He rose from his seat and kicked his chair away from him. He turned in my direction and used his left hand to hold my face while squeezing my cheeks. He held them so tightly, my teeth dug into the skin of my cheeks. My eyes bugged from my head and my breathing got heavier. My heart was pounding out of my chest, which I was pretty sure he felt against his body. I looked up at him and there was a different look in his eyes that sure as hell almost made me piss my pants.

"I said no, and that's final. Stop pouting like a damn child." Jason's eyes danced around and within seconds a smile formed on his face and he placed a kiss on my lips. Next, he simply walked away.

I didn't realize, I had been holding my breath until he'd been out of the kitchen for two minutes. The tears slipped from my eyes effortlessly. This was a major red flag but of course, at this time, I decided to ignore it. I wiped my tears away, then moved around the table collecting the abandoned dishes and began scraping the food into the garbage pail. There was a little voice in the back of my mind telling me to go and never look back, but my heart was speaking louder. Jason and I hadn't been together for a full year yet, but I loved that man more than I needed air to breathe. So, of course, my heart won, and all my senses went out of the window.

After I made sure the kitchen was spotless, I made my way upstairs to our bedroom to check up on him. He was in his boxers sitting up against the headboard. The remote was in his hand and his attention was on the screen.

"That kitchen clean?" Jason asked startling me from my gaze.

I was thrown off by his question, but I still answered. "Yes, I was coming to check on you, before I ran out to go to the grocery store for dinner and other things."

"Everything straight, make sure you go there and come straight back."

A slight smile was on my face, as I nodded and turned to head downstairs. My purse was already on the table next to the couch, I grabbed it, slipped on my Sperry skippies, and left to climb into his car. I exhaled, grabbed my phone, and tried to call Erica. She didn't answer, I needed her because Jason's actions were off, and I didn't know if I was tripping or not.

I made it to Price Chopper within five minutes and made a beeline for the meat department. I was going to make his favorite dish, which was New York strip steak smothered with onions and mushrooms, French cut green beans and homemade mashed potatoes. I didn't have to get any gravy because Jason liked the gravy I made with the steak over top the potatoes. I was in the produce aisle when I heard my name being called. I looked in the direction of the voice and to my surprise, Jason's friend Kareem was the one calling me. I'd only seen him in uniform and almost dropped the bag of potatoes I had in my hand. He was indeed looking fine dressed in simple black cargo shorts and a white T-shirt.

"Um, hey, Kareem, right?" I asked. Although he was Jason's friend, we'd only met a handful of times.

"That's right. How are you?"

"I'm good and yourself."

"I'm alive so I have no room to complain," he chuckled. "Where's Jason, he here with you?"

"No, not this time, he's home resting from working all night."

As I mentioned this a look came across his face, I couldn't decipher. Kareem noticed and decided to place a smile on his face.

"Tell Jason to hit me up so we can get caught up on some things. Oh, yeah, Quinn, you look beautiful today."

After that Kareem went about his business and left me standing there, with a huge smile on my face and my cheeks flushed. My phone ringing took me out of my trance and I cursed out the person who was interrupting my moment. Being with Jason or not, a girl who gets a compliment deserves to enjoy it. I reached into my pocket and grabbed my phone before the person decided to end the call.

"Hello," I answered.

"You called me, I was in the shower." it was Erica.

"Yeah, but it's cool, I was coming to Price Chopper and wanted the company."

"Oh, my bad girl, my boo thang was over, and he put a hurting on this thing," Erica replied with a chuckle.

"Oh, that's too much information. Anyway, while I got you on the phone, Jason and I, decided we won't be having a wedding. It would be less expensive if we were to celebrate with a dinner with our closest friends at the reception."

"Okay, cool, so instead of planning a wedding, we'll be planning a small dinner?" she questioned to make sure, she heard me right.

After all, she was helping me plan and I knew she wanted it to be just as perfect as I wanted it to be.

"Exactly."

Erica and I spoke for a few minutes longer before Jason started to blow up my phone. When I answered, he asked me what was taking so long. I let him know, I was on my way to check out and would be home soon. Hopefully, by then he'd be in a better mood. If not, then I planned on making sure he was.

Chapter Eleven

What kind of love from a nigga would
Black your eye?
What kind of love from a nigga
Every night makes you cry?
What Kind of love from a nigga
Make you wish he would die?

It was a full two weeks later when my mother was released from the hospital. My father had done quite a number on my mother. Her bruises were healing and the cuts from the plate, Daddy smashed into her face were slowly scabbing over. Donald and I were back home, and for the first night, for once it seemed everything was going to be okay. Donald and I made Mama lay in bed, while we cooked, cleaned, and basically waited on her hand and foot like she deserved. Mama informed Donald and me, that she didn't press charges against, Daddy but she also wasn't letting him back home.

"Your father has hurt me physically and emotionally for the last time. Over my dead body will that man come anywhere near us again," Was her response to Donald after he had asked if Daddy was coming back.

"Do you love him still?" I had to ask.

I needed to know because I was unsure whether I should still love him or not. What he did was fucked up beyond measures.

Mama cleared her throat before she answered me. "You know what, Sweetie? I won't sit here and say I don't, because I do. Your father was everything to me, and I don't understand where things went wrong. Now that he is away things will get better, I promise."

Donald and I took her word and believed her, because of the extent of the damages he'd done. Several years later, things were going just as Mama said they would.

***

I was weeks away from my sixteenth birthday, Mama was helping me plan my party. We were sitting at the table talking about color schemes when there was a knock on the door. Mama and I looked at each other because we knew it wasn't Donald for the simple fact, that he had a key. I shrugged my shoulders and got up to make my way to the door.

"Who is it?" I called out.

There was a long pause. "It's your, Daddy, baby girl," he finally said.

My heart sank to my feet, I moved from the door and tried to make eye contact with, Mama. I was too late, she made it to the door looking at me like I was crazy.

"Well, why are you just standing there, silly girl? Who's at the door?" she questioned.

"It's me, Gigi," my dad said through the door.

My mother looked at me and I looked back shrugging my shoulder's. I didn't know what to do because I didn't expect him to show his face again. It had been three years since anyone had spoken to or seen him. I gave my mother one last look, and made my way back to the kitchen, all the while praying she didn't open that door. I knew if she did, he would sweet talk her into letting him come back home. My Mama was weak when it came to my father, it was only easy for her to forget about him because he was the one who never reached out.

"What are you doing here, Ernest?" My mother asked as I sat at the kitchen table.

I didn't hear the locks being undone so that was a good sign.

"*Giselle, I miss you and the kids,*" my dad responded.

"*Hmph, you chose to stay gone for three years. You could have called or sent a letter to see how we were doing,*" she huffed.

I begged her in my head not to fall for it. I was about to fall to my knees and pray to God she didn't.

"*I was only away so I could get myself together, baby. I realized what I was doing to you and the kids was wrong. I was fucked up entirely, Giselle. I needed to fix myself, to be a better man to you, and a better father to the kids. Y'all are my world, I wouldn't want to keep hurting y'all. I'm sorry, baby, I just want you to see, I am a changed man.*"

Thank, God, I was in the kitchen because if Mama saw how hard I rolled my eyes, I'm pretty sure she would have smacked the taste out of my mouth. There was a long pause after my dad stopped talking. I could have sworn at that moment, I heard the locks unlocking. I sighed, stood up from the table, and began gathering my things to take up to my room. I made sure to walk past the door and eyed my dad. His eyes lit up once he saw me.

"*Baby Girl, wow, you've grown,*" my dad spoke to me.

My eyes turned into slits. "*Ernest,*" I responded, and continued to my room.

I couldn't explain how this fire of anger was burning so deeply inside of me. I used to love my dad with everything in me, but it was like the beating he put on my mama changed everything. I hoped my mother remembered and decided to close the door in his face. That was hopeful wishing because my mother never came to my room to check on me. So that only led me to believe she caved and let him in.

***

The sun was down when I woke up from an unexpected nap. The house was quiet and there was a body lying next to me. Donald finally came home from wherever he'd been and snuck in my bed. When he was worried and wanted to protect me, he would lie next to me, watching me sleep until he dozed. It had been three years exactly, since the time Daddy decided to leave, that Donald had stopped.

"Donald," I spoke, shaking him awake.

"Huh, what happened, you okay?" He asked as he jumped from his sleep.

"Yes, I'm fine, I was just waking you, to see if you wanted to go get in your bed. I'm about to turn the T.V. on, I don't want to disturb you."

Donald softened his eyes as they smiled at me instead of his lips. "You know, I can't do that. Mommy let that nigga back in. If I'm out there, all senses of him being my pops is going out the window. I'm bigger and stronger now, I can guarantee, I'll knock his ass out."

I giggled, I knew Donald would stick to his word. I laid back on my bed, looked up at the ceiling and began speaking my thoughts to Donald. "You know, I don't see how he could leave for three years. Then claim the only reason he left was, so he could get himself together. He could've done that while staying here. All we have now is his words to go by."

"I honestly feel, she just let him fuck and go," Donald added.

"Donald, eww, that's nasty."

"I'm serious, when was the last time you seen her go hang out? Or even allow another man to come in here?"

"Never."

"Exactly, hopefully, she just fucks him and kicks him out, so that our lives can go back to being our new normal."

Things between Donald and I got quiet as we were left with our own thoughts. Secretly, I hoped Mama did exactly what Donald said. We had built this new normal, and if Mama allowed Daddy to come back, it would all be in vain. Several minutes of quietness passed by, until we heard a loud 'Thud!' Donald and I sat up and looked at each other. I'm pretty sure Donald's heart was pounding in his chest, just like mine was. Our breathing was still as we expected to hear something else. Because we didn't, we laid back down.

"Aahhh—Ernest, get off me!" We heard my mother yell.

Donald and I bolted from my bed and ran from my room. They were by the stairs, where my mother's room was, and she just so happen to be on the floor.

"Get the fuck up off of her!" Donald yelled with his fists balled up.

"Y'all go back in the room!" Mama yelled from the floor.

Our father looked at us and smirked. "Your, mama, thinks she can just up and leave me again. For three years, I stayed away because I was getting myself together to be a better man for y'all. Now she doesn't want to accept my apologies," Ernest spoke.

Donald stepped closer and yelled, "I swear to God, if you don't get away from my damn mama, you gonna regret it!"

"Oh, so, you big and bad now? Let's see how much you are." With all his strength, Daddy took his fist and smashed it against Mama's face.

We heard the cracking of the bones in her face. Blood gushed from everywhere as she howled from the pain that overtook her. My mouth dropped open at the sight in front of me. Tears stung my eyes as I froze in fear. Donald was getting him good until daddy took a cheap shot and hit him in the nuts. Donald had no choice, but to stop the assault on daddy. Daddy wore a smirk on his face, as he swung at Donald, connecting with his face and knocking him out. A triumphant smirk spread across daddy's face, yet again, as I rushed over to Donald to make sure he was okay.

"Donald, get up please," I begged with tears streaming down my face.

Daddy stalked over to Mama and grabbed her up by her hair. She cried out in pain and I cried harder trying to wake Donald up as best as I could.

"Giselle, it will be a cold day in hell, before you move on without me. You took a vow, for better or for worse, till death do us part," he sneered.

Mama whimpered as she continued to hold her face. Donald finally came back to reality and shook off Daddy's hit.

"Ernest, please," Mom cried out.

Donald balled his fists up again and got ready to rush Daddy. I was so scared of what was going on in front of me. I was frozen as time slowed down. One-minute, Donald, was standing next to me, the next Daddy threw Mama down by the stairs. She tried to catch her balance, but her elbow broke as she landed on her hand to break her fall, snapped at the impact and she went tumbling down the stairs.

"Noooo!" I yelled and ran after my Mama.

I was the first one down the stairs and to her side. Her eyes were wide open but vacant. There was blood leaking from her head and face. By the look on her face, I knew she was dead. The house became quiet, momentarily. Donald let out a gut-wrenching roar as he rushed, daddy. He rained blow after blow on daddy, each blow was full of force and anger. Something finally clicked in my head, that told me to get to the phone, and call for police. When they answered, I gave them my address and a brief description of what was going on.

"Donald, stop it—Donald," I yelled.

***

"Ouch!" I yelped.

I didn't know what was going on. I was no longer in the comforts of my bed. I was on the floor and Jason was standing over me with a menacing look. I stared back with confusion written all over my face.

"Who the fuck is, Donald? Why do you feel so comfortable yelling his name out in my bed!" Jason screamed.

Before I could answer him, he used the back of his hand to strike me across my face. Tears stung my eyes as I touched my lip and blood appeared on my fingers.

"He's my brother," I rushed to get out before he even thought about hitting me again.

"What?"

"I have a brother named, Donald. I was having a nightmare from my past." I climbed off the floor and cut my eyes at Jason as I made my way to the bathroom, to observe the damage he'd done.

Jason followed close behind me. "I'm so sorry, babe. I didn't know."

I mumbled, "How could you if I never told you?"

"I know, I'm sorry."

"You hit me."

"I don't know, what came over me. It won't happen again." Jason grabbed a washcloth, wet it in cold water, and placed it on my lip.

My mother's voice echoed in my head telling me to run. That if I stayed it was only going to get worse. Jason kissed my lip where it was now swollen. I looked him in his eyes to see if he was sincere. Hurt and regret danced in his eyes and my heart had already forgiven him. Jason continued to kiss me, as he moved down south. I was dressed only in a silk gown and thin lace panties. Jason lifted my nightgown and ripped my panties off with one tug. He threw one of my legs over his shoulder and slid his finger up and down between my slit.

All was forgotten for the moment, as his tongue connected with my clit. I scooted onto the sink, so he could have a better advantage at getting all my juices. My head fell back against the mirror as ecstasy engulfed me.

"I'm sorry, babe, I love you," Jason whispered against my pussy.

I moaned that he was forgiven. My heart beat hard in my chest, as I felt his tongue flicked against my clit. My fingers turned white as I gripped the sides of the sink and felt my juices releasing on his tongue.

"My God, Jason, I forgive you!" I yelled as my body shook.

Jason moved his face from between my legs and looked up at me with a smile on his face. Jason placed his lips against mine as I tasted myself on him. I pulled his pants from his hips as his tongue got familiar with my neck. I pulled his dick from his pants and guided it to my love nest. As his head entered me, my mouth dropped, as my pussy fit his length just right. Jason pulled my nightie down over my breast and popped my nipple into his mouth, sucking on it like he was a newborn nursing.

My head banged against the wall as Jason moved his pelvis, so his manhood dove in and out of me. He wrapped his hand around my neck, and my pussy dripped wetness that made noises as he moved in me faster.

"Ma, I'm about to cum," Jason whispered in my ear. "Let me put a baby in you," he continued.

My eyes shot open, due to the surprise request he just laid on me. "Are you sure?"

"Yes, babe, we about to be married, why not start our family? You trust me, right? Say, yes, please cause this nut is right there," Jason said with a chuckle.

"Yes baby," I agreed.

Although I was a little skeptical about it, I still agreed. He had a point, but I knew there was something behind it. Jason's face nestled into my neck, as he paused deep up in me, letting his seeds go. After we cleaned up, we joined each other in bed and fell into sleeping bliss.

~Erica~

The nightmares I was having were new. What I had done several years ago was coming back to haunt me. I hated to fall asleep and cocaine became my new best friend, just so I wouldn't have to deal with the night-mares. No matter what I did though, they still seemed to show up.

The sun was shining bright and for the first time in a while, I slept somewhat good. I climbed out of my mas-sive bed, stood in front of the vanity style dresser and looked at my naked body while I stretched. Instantly, I felt disgusted, the bleaching soap I'd been using for weeks now, had not made a difference in my skin com-plexion. I was still as dark as fudge. I just wanted my skin to be a little lighter. I sucked my teeth, and made my way to the bathroom, to shower and get ready to have break-fast with Quinn.

I continued to use the skin lightening soap even though, I wasn't seeing any changes. It was supposed to be the best out there, so I'd just wait it out a bit longer. I wasn't going to lose hope just yet. I dried off as I walked into my room, then cleansed my body in moisturizer and began getting dressed. It was fall in 2017, and it was just a tad nippy outside, so I opted to put on a pair of blue ripped jeans, brown, leather, lace-up, combat military an-kle boots, and a crème colored sweater. I parted my hair in the middle and slicked it into a knot bun and placed in my drawstring ponytail. Then threw in my diamond stud earrings and grabbed my blue jean jacket and black Steve Madden purse.

I caught an Uber to Denny's on Nott Terrace. When I arrived, Quinn was sitting in the waiting area. I rolled my eyes as I noticed, we were somewhat dressed the same. Her jeans were black as well as her boots, she had on a white T-shirt, and a black flight jacket with her ensemble. Her hair was in a ponytail and braided down instead of the usual puff she rocked.

"Girl, you, must have been looking in my window this morning," I spoke as I approached causing her to take her eyes off her phone.

"Nooo, great minds just think alike. But, I see you, you look amazing."

I spun around and said, "Why, thank you, are you ready to be seated?"

"Sure," Quinn responded.

The hostess handed us our menus and we followed her to the booth we'd be sitting at. Once we were seated, we started off with cups of coffee and our waiter gave us a few minutes to look over our menus.

Quinn began, "These last few months have felt like things have changed. Like we barely have any time to hang out, with each other anymore."

"Well, that's because you went and got into a relationship."

"Oh, no, ma'am this is not even all on me. If I remember not too long after Jason and I got together, you got together with your boo thang."

I giggled only because she was right on a certain level. She just didn't know it was her husband. "Yes, I will give you that."

"Okay, then, don't just try and blame it on me. By the way, when am I going to meet the guy who's putting a smile on your face."

"Soon enough, I just want to make sure this thing is real, you know? I don't want to introduce him to anybody until I know we are official, and things are going somewhere."

"I know what you mean, girl. You have to make sure there is more than just a sexual connection."

"That, I know," I recanted.

The waiter came back and we both decided on pancakes, bacon, sausage, eggs, home fries, and another coffee. While we caught up, she asked my opinion of emerald green and white as the color scheme for her and Jason's reception dinner. Of course, I was in my feelings about it, but I had to play my part. While playing my part, I was trying to devise a plan, so Jason wouldn't marry, Quinn. Hell, I was the better woman for him on so many levels. Not saying that Quinn can't, but I can throw down with the greatest chefs in the world, clean as if I was a maid, and let's not forget, I can fuck him like a pornstar. Jason was the man for me and best friend or not, he was going to be mine at the end of the day.

"Erica, did you hear me?" Quinn questioned, as she noticed my far-off stare.

Shit, I was daydreaming about Jason sucking on this clit and it had my nipples erect and my panties wet.

"I'm sorry, no I didn't, my mind was somewhere else at the moment."

"I said Jason wants to start having kids, but I'm not sure how to feel about it."

It felt like my heart stop beating in my chest. I wondered when he made this decision because he spoke to me about everything. Why would he do this? My silence was eating at Quinn because she looked at me with her eyes wide waiting for me to say something.

'Think of something to say, Erica,' I coached myself.

My eyes searched hers to see if she was playing a trick on me or not, then it clicked.

I placed my knife and fork onto my plate, cleared my throat, and said, "For me, I think, y'all should start a family as soon as possible. It's nothing like bringing life into the world. But, you might want to reconsider if you want to marry him and bring a child into an abusive relationship. Tell me Quinn, is that ketchup or blood slightly oozing from that gash on the side of your lip?"

She eyed me as she went inside of her purse, extracting a compact mirror. I averted my eyes as she checked on her lip. Did I have to go there? Of course not, but I needed her to come down a couple of notches. Jason hadn't told me about any abuse going on and I pushed it by accusing Jason of putting his hands on her, but if it was true, I knew it would sting.

"If you are implying that Jason—"

"I did imply, I said if you want to bring a baby into an abusive relationship then go for it."

"Jason isn't abusive, Erica if you must know. So, you can stop reaching."

"Are you sure, cause that busted lip is telling me something different?"

Quinn shook her head with a smirk on her face. "If you must know, I was having a nightmare from the night my mama died, and ended up rolling from the bed, landing face first onto the floor."

If that was the story, she was going to tell then so be it. Both Quinn and I, to her knowledge knew I had never been in their bedroom. She didn't know, I knew they had plush floor-to-floor carpeting in their bedroom.

I threw my hands up as if I was surrendering. "If that's the story, you're sticking too, so be it. You are acting like I've never seen signs of abuse. I mean, after all, we are best friends."

"And just what the fuck is that supposed to mean?" Quinn questioned.

I knew I'd hit her below the belt, but I needed her to hurt and go home venting Jason. Jason would eventually get tired of her complaining and come to my place.

"You of all people should see the signs of domestic violence. I figured seeing the shit growing up, you'd know the signs." I knew, I was pushing it but I didn't care.

I could tell Quinn was damn near in tears but surprisingly, she kept it together.

"You're supposed to be my best friend, but you feel it's okay to say some shit like that to my face? Knowing how sensitive that is to me?" Quinn questioned in a shaky voice.

"Look, Quinn, I know you and Jason are in love and about to be married, but you don't deserve what he's doing to you."

"And what exactly is he doing? You just said my family business loud and in public. So, obviously you know, I know the signs and I'm telling you he's not putting his hands on me!" Quinn yelled causing the whole restaurant to turn their attention on us.

"Quinn, lower your voice. I'm just being a concerned friend."

"A concerned friend? You straight up assumed. You didn't ask questions. You didn't care what came out of your mouth, and you brought up my family situation, knowing how hard it is for me to deal with!"

"You act like you don't know how I give it up. Straight with no chaser."

Quinn was hurt, but I didn't care. Her eyes turned to slits as she stared me down as if she was hoping I'd spontaneously combust. I picked up my fork and knife and continued eating my meal. That was until I was blinded with pain. My hand shot up to my face and I opened my eyes to see blood dripping through my fingers and onto my plate. My eyesight was doubled, but I did see Quinn storming off. Maybe I should have cared about taking it too far.

~Quinn~

I couldn't believe Erica! I was hurt and more importantly, I was pissed. Who did she think she was talking to like that? She knew she was by bringing up a sensitive subject. The tears ran hot down my face like it was pouring from the sky. I even began to hyperventilate as I speed walked up the block towards downtown. My mind wasn't working because I could have easily gotten into my car, but my thinking process was off.

"Excuse, me miss," I heard a female calling for me.

I turned around thinking it was a waitress from Denny's and I was ready to throw down if need be. It wasn't, instead, I saw a very pretty woman who looked like she was dipped in the richest chocolate. Her skin was flawless, and her body was banging. I watched as her thick thighs swayed my way, her hair blowing in the wind.

"Yes?" I asked as I used my sleeve on my shirt to wipe away my tears.

"I heard and saw what happened in Denny's. I can assure you, I am not trying to be Nosey Rosey, but I am deeply sorry you are going through this. I can see you are in a great deal of pain. What your so-called friend said back there was a bunch of low blows and I know her kind well. Do you mind if I ask you a question?"

"I mean, do I seriously have a choice? You done heard all of my business back there."

"Does the Jason you and your friend were talking about happen to be, Jason Braxton, in the army?"

My eyes turned into slits and I grew angry, yet again. *'If this bitch tells me she's fucking him, all hell about to break loose.'* I thought, balling my fists "Why?"

She noticed my hands balled up. She stretched her arms out in front of her. Her arms were a plea while her face said not to fuck with her. "Trust me, it's not what you're thinking. Jason and I dated before. I'm pretty sure he has told you the story about the girl who left him for his cousin and the whole baby thing, right?"

"He has." I eyed her skeptically.

"None of that is true. I only know he's telling women these stories because women after me, would seek me out and verbally drag me for leaving him. He is very abusive and dangerous. I did have a baby and it was by his cousin, but that was way after he and I broke up. Jason needs serious help before he seriously hurts somebody."

"Why are you telling me this?"

"Because what I saw back there used to be me. I would take up for him knowing what he was doing was wrong. If I could have had a friend like yours, even if she was being a bitch about it, she truly seemed concerned. You should get out while you can. Before you end up scared or worse." She lifted her shirt and showed me a long stab wound on her side.

My mouth dropped because in my mind there was no way Jason could have done that. Could he? I know he's been aggressive with me, but was he capable of attempting to kill someone? She warned me one more time to get out while I can, then walked away. If my mind wasn't cloudy before it was damn sure fuzzy now. My tears were now dried, and I made my way to my car. The ambulance was there bringing Erica out on a stretcher. Just like I saw her, she saw me, too. I climbed into my car and made my way back home.

When I arrived, Jason's car was in the garage and everything his ex-told me and what happened between Erica and me at Denny's infuriated me. I climbed out of the car and slammed the door behind me, almost shattering the window. I walked inside the house on a mission to find,

Jason. When I found him, he was in the kitchen fixing a sandwich, while on the phone.

"We need to talk, now!" I yelled.

Jason looked at me over his shoulder like I was crazy.

"I'll be there as soon as I can. I'll call you, to let you know when I'm on my way," Jason spoke into the phone, then hung up.

"You see this shit on my lip! I thought I could forgive you for it, but after my best friend threw it in my face, causing me to rock her shit, I don't think I can! After the first time, when you squeezed my cheeks. I should have packed my shit then. I saw my mama get her ass whooped by my daddy until he killed her! I refuse to go down that route!" My chest burned, and my eyes stung as I expressed myself to Jason.

He stood against the counter eating his sandwich, watching me attentively. My stomach turned as I watched him standing there, just looking at me. It was long silent five minutes as he just stood slowly eating his sandwich. Once he was done, he dusted his hands off and walked in my direction. He cuffed my chin and his eyes turned to something dark.

"Do what I say and be the good wife, I know you can be and I won't kill you." Holding his gaze for a few seconds longer, he moved from me.

Was he serious? My body shook with terror as the way he looked at me kept playing in my mind.

He came back into the kitchen fully dressed and said, "Have dinner ready. I should be back no later than seven." A smile was plastered on his face, then he kissed my forehead, and walked out the door.

The words of his ex's warning wouldn't leave my mind. But still, I decided to stay. For one, he gave me a life I never thought I would have. Granted I'd had jobs, but I was never able to hold one long enough to move up and get off welfare. Two, and most importantly, I loved him for it. I loved him so much, I didn't let what he said faze me. I ignored the red flags because love blinded me. I was sure things would be better.

"He's probably stressing at work and this is just a slight hiccup," that's what I told myself every time things got rough.

MIMI

Chapter Twelve

Your face will be the reason I smile
But I will not see what I cannot
Have forever
I'll always love you, I hope you feel
The same

~Three Months Later~

January 18ᵗʰ, 2018 marked the day I was married to Jason. Through the three months, we'd have some hiccups, but we would be back to being in love only hours after what we went through passed. It was Saturday, January 20ᵗʰ and I was getting ready for our reception dinner. Jason and I were in the same hotel, the Marriott in Albany. We were in two separate rooms and once he was done getting ready. He was heading down to the ballroom, then he'd call up to my room, so I could come down.

I sat in front of the mirror and covered the slightly, black eye that was slowly healing from a week before. A flashback of me standing beside my mother, as she did the same thing I was doing played in my head. A tear willed itself to fall from my eye, but I brushed that away and placed a smile on my face. I stood up and looked at myself in the full-length mirror, I'd brought from my house just for this reason. I looked flawless, I was dressed in an emerald green, off the shoulder mermaid dress with a train.

Around my neck was a diamond choker with a tassel dipped down between my breasts. A diamond bangle rested on my right wrist, my diamond and platinum engagement ring and wedding band rested in my left hand.

My hair was in a cascade of curls and although I was hiding a bruise, my make-up was light and natural looking. On my feet were peep toe stiletto's that had a vine of leaves going up the heel and back of the shoe made up of emeralds and crystals. I looked good and I smiled as I looked at the dress hugging every curve.

As I admired myself, there was a knock on my door. When I went over to answer it, I was surprised to see it was Kareem. He looked good in his all-white tux and shoes. An emerald green handkerchief sat in his tuxedo jacket, breast pocket and a green bow tie rested at the base of his neck. His hair was freshly cut and lined like Jesus had done it himself.

"Wow," Kareem expressed.

My face immediately turned hot and I'm pretty sure he was genuine with his shock.

"Ka—Kareem, what are you doing here?" I stammered.

Kareem looked me up and down before he answered, "Oh um, Jason asked me to come get you. He said Erica showed up and is asking for your forgiveness or something like that."

I sucked my teeth instantly and turned my back to check my make-up one last time. I opened my mouth to begin, but quickly shut it and burst into tears. I sat on the chair and Kareem rushed in and closed the door behind him. He rushed to my side and rubbed my back.

"What's wrong?" he asked sincerely.

"All of these people here are Jason's friends and family. Erica is my only friend slash family member, and I don't want her here."

"She made sure to put whatever y'all are going through aside for your day. Maybe you should reconsider her presence."

He was right. Did I want to admit it? Hell no, but I dried my eyes anyway and reapplied my makeup.

"What's up with your eye?" Kareem asked looking at me through the mirror.

"Nothing," I answered, quickly applying some more foundation.

"It's fading but I know I saw a bruise."

I sighed and answered, "Jason and I were talking, cracking jokes on each other. When I turned to grab a cup from the cabinet, I walked smack into the cabinet door. It's fine."

Kareem looked at me in disbelief. There was a long pregnant pause before Kareem said, "My mother was in an abusive relationship after my father left. I've heard the *'I ran into the cabinet'* excuse plenty of times repeatedly. Over the past few months, I think we've become close enough for me to say, Erica isn't your only friend here. And another thing, I don't care how long I've known, Jason, if you need me to beat his ass, just say the word. Now grab what you need and let's get you downstairs."

I smiled at his kind words and got up from my seat. Kareem's face had a smile displayed but I peeped his jaw tightening. We walked to the elevator and waited in silence. My heart was beating through my chest, I was more nervous about this dinner than I was to say I do.

"By the way, you look amazing *if I* was in Jason's shoes, you'd have nothing to worry about. For now, I'll leave it alone," Kareem spoke, making sure he emphasized if he was in Jason's shoes.

We climbed into the elevator and made it downstairs to the ballroom. Once we got to the doors he told me to stay put as he went to let Jason know I was downstairs. It took Kareem five minutes to come and get me, by that time, I was floating on air because of all the compliments from everyone that passed me. Cloud nine had replaced my bad mood and I refused to complain.

Kareem peeked his head through the door with a smile and asked if I was ready. I took a deep breath, exhaled, placed a smile on my face, and nodded yes. Kareem swung the double doors open and I was taken aback by the decorations. I willed my feet to move as *'Pretty Wings'* by *'Maxwell'* began to play. The tables were covered in satin, emerald green tablecloths, white plates sat on top of the tables, and white, lily green bells sat in vases in the middle of the tables. The chairs were draped in white satin chair covers with emerald green cloth, tied around the chairs into a bow in the back.

Tears couldn't help but coat the rim of my eyes after taking in all the decorations. I finally spotted Jason up at the table where we were to sit at. My breath was taken away at how handsome he looked. His suit was white just like all the men, but there was just something about the white that mixed so well with his milk chocolate complexion. A smile adorned his face and if I squinted just right, I could for sure see he'd been holding back a few tears himself. At that moment, whatever we were going through, didn't exist.

It seemed like forever in a lifetime for me to reach my husband. I placed a kiss on his lips and we smiled at each other.

Jason spoke first, "I now feel like an asshole for telling you no to a wedding. If I knew you were going to look this beautiful, I would have said, yes."

I threw my head back in laughter and responded, "I'm glad you did suggest it. We had our private moment and now we can share it with our family and friends."

"You know what, you are right, I won't lie. Come, let's take our seats." Jason grabbed my hand as we walked around the table to take our seat.

At the far end of the table, sat our wedding cake. It was simple but beautiful. It was a three-tiered cake and had green flowers wrapped up and around the cake. The D.J. was cutting up with some old school Hip Hop and R&B from the 90s. My favorite music era.

An hour passed and after taking multiple pictures, I remembered Erica was there. I looked through the throngs of people to see if I could spot her. When I did she was sitting in a corner of the room with her phone in her hand. From where I sat, I noticed she looked different. She'd dyed her hair almost like my golden-brown color and her skin looked a little lighter as well. I told Jason I was going to speak with Erica. His jaw tightened as he nodded, and I made my way over to her.

"Erica, thank you for coming. It means a lot to me," I spoke as I walked up on her. Indeed, her skin was lighter than usual, but she was still dark.

Erica looked up with a smile and patted the seat next to her. "I wouldn't have missed it for the world. Even if you didn't want me here," she said.

I giggled and began to apologize, "I'm sorry about what happened at Denny's. I was wrong for putting my hands on you—"

Erica shook her head and cut me off, "No it was my fault. Me and bae were having an off week, I took it out in you. I shouldn't have done that, I'm sorry."

"Hug it out?"

"That's what we do best."

For the remainder of the night, everyone enjoyed themselves with dancing, good food, and drinks. My face began to hurt from smiling and laughing so much. By eleven, people were good and drunk heading home. Erica volunteered to stay behind with Kareem and Jason to help the staff clean up. I went home to shower and slip into something more comfortable for my husband, that he never got to see because he decided not to come home.

~Erica~

As I left Quinn's dinner, I had a lot on my mind. My initial intentions were to help Kareem and Jason clean up with the staff, but Jason told me to go home and get some rest. During our conversation, I knew Kareem was watching us, I'm pretty sure he'd put two and two together sooner than later. Once, I got home, I tooted a little bit of coke to work up the nerve to text Jason and tell him that what we had, needed to end. I felt super guilty about how we were doing Quinn. She was a good person and didn't deserve this kind of betrayal from us.

Jason, first, I want to say that I love you with all my heart. I want you to know that the time we've shared was very special. I truly don't want it to end, but I've had some time to think. I realized that what we're doing behind Quinn's back is wrong. I think our time has run its course and, in my heart, I know, I can't do this no more. I wish we had met under different terms and that it was me you met first. I will always love you, but tonight is the last night we will see each other! ~Erica~

I knew he wouldn't like it, but my loyalty should have been solely to her and not him. I thought maybe because she didn't know about Jason and me, I could probably keep this hidden and she'd never find out. After I sent the text message, I put my phone on the table next to my bed and went to watch a movie in the living room. Eventually, the movie began to watch me because I zoned out and went back to a time in my life, that I regretted every day of my life.

I was seventeen, still trying to figure out my life as a teenager. Daddy had left mommy, myself, and my little sister because my momma's abuse was not only extended to me, but to him as well. When he left, I resented him because he didn't take me and my sister. Well shit, just me, my sister was light-skinned, so she didn't get abused at all. In fact, everything was handed to that bitch on a silver platter dipped in diamonds. My sister and I used to have a good relationship until she got old enough, and my mother began to taint her and make her abuse me like she would.

I remembered this day like it was yesterday. My mom had left to run errands and left me in the house with my sister. Because of our estranged relationship, I kept myself locked in my room. Soon after my mother left, I found myself feeling tired, so I took a nap. Before I knew it, my mother came back and woke me from my slumber by throwing a mop bucket filled with dirty water on me, then began whipping me with a belt.

"Aahhh, what did I do?" I cried.

My body was in so much pain as I tried to dodge my mother's belt.

"You, ungrateful black burnt, bitch! How dare you?" She yelled every time the belt connected with my skin.

"What did I do—what did I do?"

"So, your black ass gonna sit there and act like you ain't make all of those dishes in that sink, huh?"

"Mama, I didn't, I stayed in my room and slept while you were gone."

She raised her arm to swing on me again, but she hesitated. Instead, she called my sister into the room. Once my sister was there she asked, "Who put all them dishes in that sink?"

For once, I thought that she was going to take my side. My sister looked from me to my mama and back again. She opened her mouth when she saw that my mother decided to move closer to her with the belt.

My sister belted, "Mama, it was Erica, she had that girl, Quinn, over here and made some of your good bacon for them! She told me not to tell or else you would whoop me, too!"

My mouth dropped at what Ashley had just said. Not caring that my mother was still standing there, I charged at Ashley.

I ran over my bed and yelled, "You, little lying, wench!"

I came inches away from snatching her by her hair when my mama stepped in and clotheslined me. I instantly dropped to the floor holding my throat. My mother stepped over me with disgust on her face. Tears from all the years of being hurt, by the one person that was supposed to love me the most, surfaced. I didn't understand why she hated me so much.

"You gonna get in that kitchen and clean that motherfucker. And if you got a problem with it you can leave my house," my mother huffed.

Although I was hurt, I wasn't about to clean something up that wasn't my fault. I cried my last bit of tears, stood up from the floor, and stared my mother in her eyes. After a few challenging seconds, I grabbed a suitcase, began packing my things, took my sister by the arm and left my room. I was finished in minutes and out of the door. I didn't know where I was going so I just sat in front of the building. Hours had passed before I came up with a plan. The sky was dark, and I looked at the time on my phone. Time had gone by so fast, that it was approaching midnight. I knew my mother and sister would be sleeping. I dragged my suitcase back upstairs, stuck my key in the door and made my way around the house as quiet as a church mouse.

I went inside the kitchen and grabbed a knife. At the time, I wasn't thinking about the consequences. I just wanted them out of my life for being the reason for all my hurt. I wasn't thinking straight, I went into my sister's room first and stood by her bed watching her sleep with the knife handle in both hands. I plunged the knife deep through her, causing her to die instantly. No fight. No nothing. A sickening smile came across my face as I struggled to take the knife out of her chest cavity. Next up was my mother. I walked into her room with the knife dripping blood at my feet.

My mother was snoring loudly as I approached her bed.

'How could she sleep so peacefully, knowing just hours ago, she'd kicked me out? Not knowing if I was okay or not,' I thought.

It sickened me to know, I'd been born from such an evil person. I raised my hands and plunged the knife deep into her stomach and watched as her eyes sprang open. When she looked from the knife to my face, shock registered as she tried to talk.

"You were supposed to protect me and love me, but all you've done is hurt me and humiliate me. How could you do such a thing to your child? How could you be so evil? All my life, I just wanted your love and affection, and you hated me because of the color of my skin. Do you know, I now hate myself because of all of the things you put me through?"

As she tried to speak, blood began to spill from her mouth, but the only thing I heard was her calling Ashley's name. She couldn't even tell me, she was sorry. I leaned closer to her and whispered that Ashley was dead just like she was about to be. I twisted the knife inside her stomach and watched as her face registered pain. Tears raced down her face as I pulled the knife from her stomach. I wiped the blade on her sheets and walked out. Never looking back.

Once again, I found myself on the bench with my suitcase, not knowing where to go. The only person I could call was Pearl and so I did.

"Hello?" Quinn answered after the phone had rung five times.

I knew it was late and that she would be sleep but I needed her help.

"Quinn, I did something, and I need your help."

"I'm tired, Erica, can this wait until the morning?"

"Unless you want me behind bars, I suggest you come now."

"What did you do?" There was now urgency in her voice and it sounded like she was moving around finding her clothes.

I didn't answer, I just hung up because I knew that would light a fire under her ass and get her to me. Ten minutes later, I saw Quinn speed walking around the corner with her phone to her ear. She was calling me for the hundredth time.

"Took you long enough," I stated when she walked up.

"Why wouldn't you pick up if your phone was in your hand this whole time?" Quinn asked out of breath.

"I couldn't talk about it over the phone."

"Well, what did you do?"

"I killed them."

Quinn's eyes popped open and she cleared her throat. "You did what now—killed who?" she asked.

"My mama and Ashley, I killed both of them." I pulled the knife from my suitcase to show Quinn.

There was still traces of blood on it. Her mouth dropped as she examined the blade while it was still in my hand., Quinn began pacing back and forth mumbling to herself. Five minutes of that, she finally clapped her hands together and sat next to me.

"I can't go to jail, and neither can you. You know this whole shit with my mama passing is new and emotionally, I am dealing with a lot. I have a plan and it might work. Let's take a walk right quick, I'll tell you what's on my mind."

Quinn grabbed me by the hand and we began walking along Crane Street. We must have walked four blocks to the Family Dollar near the corner of Main Ave. Quinn told me to take the knife out of my suitcase and throw it *in the sewer. After wiping my prints off, I did what she told me to do. We began to walk back to my house and when we got there, I was supposed to call the police and explain that I'd gotten into an argument with my mother and she kicked me out. Then I was supposed to tell them after spending a few hours with Quinn, she convinced me to go home and apologize, even if I did nothing wrong. But all of that went out of the window once we got back to my apartment. There were cops everywhere, my nerves wouldn't settle, and I didn't know what to do at that point. Quinn held my hand and told me to stick to the plan, but to switch up the end, because now I wasn't the one who called the police.*

When I saw the stretchers with my mother and sister on them, I screamed and broke down. I played my part to a tee. An officer came over and began questioning Quinn and me. To this day, I don't remember exactly what I said for them to believe me. Eventually, their case was closed because there wasn't enough evidence and they couldn't link a suspect or a weapon.

***

Every time I think about that day, I automatically feel guilty because of how I've treated Quinn throughout the years. Now I've been sleeping with her husband damn near as long as they have been together. Quinn doesn't deserve a friend like me. So, I made the decision that after I ended things with Jason, I would come clean. Being that she knows what I did to my mother and sister, would it be the best option? She could easily go to the police and tell on me just to get revenge. But at this point, I didn't care. I just wanted to put it out in the open and move past it. I'd deal with the consequences later.

"What are you in here crying for?" Jason asked scaring the shit out of me. I had been so caught up in my thoughts, I didn't hear him come in.

I wiped my tears and answered, "I was thinking about something. What are you doing here? You didn't get my text?"

Jason started taking his shoes off as he sat down next to me on the couch. He grabbed at his bow tie and answered, "Nah, my phone died before I even left the hotel. My charger is at home. What's up, what was the text about?"

Everything in me didn't want to have to tell him face-to-face. It was so easy to send him that text. I saw that my cup was empty and made my way into the kitchen to make me another drink.

'Better now than never,' I thought.

Jason was still sitting on the couch when I walked back into the living room. I stood against the door frame, staring at him, debating whether I should tell him about the text or not.

"Jason, the text basically said, you and I can't do this anymore. Quinn doesn't deserve this, and I don't want to play this role any longer," I finally blurted out.

Jason lazily turned his head in my direction and chuckled. "Girl get the fuck on with that bullshit."

"No, I'm dead ass serious. Quinn is my best friend, the only person that truly cares and have love for me. I'm tired of doing her like this, it ain't right."

"Don't do this tonight, I've had a long day. I want to lay down."

"Go home and lay down with your wife."

Jason's jaw tightened as I looked at him. I didn't want any beef. He didn't respond, and I was tired, so I threw my hands up in frustration, and told him he knew where the door was, and how to use it. Then I kindly took my ass to bed. I wasn't about to get into any of his shenanigans because I was exhausted.

I climbed into bed and prayed for the first time in years. I prayed for forgiveness. I prayed for God to heal me from self-hatred, the demons that I'd been battling with coke, and I asked that God placed forgiveness in Quinn's heart when she found out what Jason and I had been doing behind her back. After my prayer, I snuggled under my blanket and prepared for a good night's sleep.

That was until I felt tugging at my hair. Next thing I knew, I was on the floor with Jason standing over me. His eyes had this dark look and I grew afraid after my initial confusion had gone away. His hand was still wrapped in my hair and his other hand was balled into a fist.

"Jason let go of my hair, you're hurting me," I said in a shaky voice.

I could tell anything I said was going through one ear and out the other. He raised his foot and kicked me in my stomach, I knew instantly he'd fucked up a couple of my ribs. The pain was unbearable.

"You came to me in the beginning. You wanted this between us. Now you're going to continue what we have, and you're not going to tell Quinn about anything. Do you understand me? So, help me God, this won't be the end of ass whooping's for you?"

"So, what you gonna do? Beat my ass like you're doing Quinn?"

"Is that what she told you?"

"She didn't have to, I saw her busted lip."

Jason laughed deep from his gut like I'd said something funny. "Do what I say, you're gonna continue like this night didn't happen and we'll be good. Do you understand Erica? During our time together, I've grown to love you. I can't picture my life without you. You play a role in my life," he replied.

"Okay, Jason, I get it. Just please let me get up."

Finally, his eyes softened, and he let my hair go. I held my stomach, sat on the edge of my bed, and struggled to breathe. Jason sat down next to me and rubbed his hand up and down my thigh. I looked at him and wondered what could possibly be going on in his head. This was not the Jason I knew. This was someone totally different.

"I'm sorry," Jason retorted, breaking the silence.

"I don't think, I can accept that apology. At least not until you show me, you won't do this again. Unlike Quinn, I won't tolerate this."

"I was diagnosed with schizophrenia."

"What?" I questioned.

I'd heard what he said, but him confessing it took me for a loop. That was something I wasn't expecting. The room was silent because I didn't know what to say. Finally, I was able to find my words. "Does Quinn know?"

"No."

"This is a big pill to swallow."

Jason sighed and said, "I know, it was for me too when I first found out. I was in denial, that is why I was discharged from the army. Since then, that's when everything began to spiral out of control. Nothing ever seems like it makes sense anymore."

"Are you taking medication for it?"

"I have it, but, I haven't started taking it yet. Do you know how that makes me feel? To go my whole life living what I felt was like a normal life, to have to rely on medication."

"Maybe seeing a therapist would help." I swung my legs onto the bed and got back under the covers.

"A therapist, no thank you."

"It might work, Jason. You might find it helpful. Don't just throw the thought down the drain."

Jason exhaled. He looked like he was defeated. He started blinking slowly. "I'll think about it, right now, I just want some rest," he said.

I patted the bed, Jason got out of his clothes and into the spot next to me. Almost instantly, he was out like a light. Before I found sleep, I battled whether I should continue to deal with Jason, to help him through his tough time, or just leave him and let him battle it on his own. I knew what I was going to do before my eyes closed for the night.

MIMI

Chapter Thirteen

It might seem crazy what I'm about to say
Sunshine she's here, you can take a break
I'm a hot air balloon that could go to space
With the air like I don't care baby by the way

~Jason~

Valentine's Day was always a holiday, I've hated. It seemed like I was alone either because I had just gotten out of a relationship, had been out of one for some time, or I was in a relationship, and we were two stubborn mules that didn't speak to each other. This Valentine's Day was different though. Although Quinn and I had been married for a month and together ultimately eight months. I felt like we had known each other for a lifetime. I have been the shittiest person to her and she didn't deserve it. She was such a sweet, caring, and kind-hearted person. I didn't understand, why I did the things that I've done. I wanted to be the man that she deserves. Maybe I should seek therapy like Erica suggested. I didn't want to be this person.

Quinn had decided to go out for the day to get pampered after a doctor's visit she had. I told her, I didn't have anything planned, and that I just wanted to chill and watch a movie on HBO. I know she was disappointed, but she agreed anyway. That was far from what exactly was going to happen. Once, she'd left the house, I cleaned the house from top to bottom with disinfectant, bleach, ammonia, the works. Once, I was done the whole house smelled brand new. I'm pretty sure you could eat off the floor.

After that was done, I'd worked up an appetite, so I made a quick run to Burger King. I sat in front of my house and ate my food so that I wouldn't make a mess in the house, after all the hard work I'd just put in. Erica kept calling me, but she knew what today was, she also knew tomorrow was her day, side-chick day. Yes, I know, I cheated on Quinn but that damn sure didn't mean, I was going to spend lover's day with my side-piece. She could be mad all she wanted.

After I was done with my meal, I went into the house and made my way to the kitchen. Next on the agenda was cooking dinner. I was making baked chicken leg quarters with tomatoes, garlic, and onions, with lemon garlic bow ties, and an apple pie cheesecake for dessert and I was mixing up Henny coladas. I was going to make sure she felt appreciated.

By the time everything was done, it was almost five, Quinn called and informed me she would be home in half an hour. The table was set with a white tablecloth and pink and red rose petals rested on top of the table. There were red candles in gold candle holders and our plates were red and white. The food was in the oven lowered down to make sure it stayed warm. I was making sure everything was perfect. Lastly, I ran upstairs to shower and get dressed. I dressed in a simple pair of slacks, a short-sleeved collared shirt, dress shoes, and my diamond faced Rolex. Quinn's dress I'd ordered her had arrived a few days prior and was hanging up in the closet along with some new shoes.

Tonight, I was going all out for my baby. Quinn's text letting me know she was pulling into the driveway, lit a fire under my ass. I got up from the couch with a hundred red, white, and pink roses. I was proud of myself for putting all this work in, a smile creased my face.

"Oh, my God!" Quinn yelled when she opened the door and saw me standing there holding the roses.

I peeked my head around the flowers and was blown away. Her hair was what women called *'romance curls'*, her make-up was flawless, and she looked like she was ready for a photo shoot. All she had to do was put on the dress I'd gotten her, and she would be set.

"Wow, you look amazing," I said in amazement.

Quinn blushed, thanked me and grabbed the roses. After smelling them Quinn said, "I really appreciate all of this. I thought we were going to just chill and watch a movie?"

"I thought that I could Jazz it up just a tad bit. I know I've been nothing but an asshole lately. I just wanted you to have this special day filled with love. Quinn, I know like hell that I am not the greatest husband, but I love you with everything in my body."

A tear slid from her eye and she hurriedly wiped it away. I placed the roses on the coffee table and wrapped my arms around Quinn. Her body melted into mine as I took in her scent of freshly washed hair.

"I love you too, Jason, and—"

"No talking. I have a surprise for you upstairs. Just go jump in the shower, when you're done look in the closet, and you'll find your surprise," I spoke showing all thirty-two of my teeth.

Quinn made her way up the stairs and I couldn't help but watch as her hips swayed from side to side. My dick jumped in my pants as I thought about diving deep inside of her. When she disappeared at the top, I made my way into the kitchen, began taking the food out of the oven and placed it nicely on our plates.

Fifteen minutes later, I was busy making sure everything was perfect. I didn't notice Quinn had made her way downstairs. I smelled her perfume before I saw her, it caused my dick to jump again. I stopped putting the final touches on the cheesecake, and when I turned around, I was blown away. The dress I'd chosen for her, was a knee-length navy blue dress, that had a stripe detail on her waist, and dipped low in a V-shape to show a little bit of cleavage. The shoes I chose were black open-toed stilettos with a gold ankle strap. After I was done accessing her from head to toe, I finally looked up at her and saw that she had a nervous look on her face.

"How do I look?" She asked as she did a full spin and flung her hair over her shoulder.

"You look breathtaking. I'm kind of at a last for words baby. You look damn good," I expressed.

Quinn giggled, made her way over towards me and wrapped her arms around me. "Thank you, baby."

"You deserve it. Take a seat and let's enjoy dinner. You know as I was getting this together, I thought maybe we could do this at least once a month. Just so we can start getting a renewal on things."

"I think that would be a good idea. There are a million and one ways to make our relationship feel new. Dinner smells and looks good, let's eat."

Over dinner, we talked about everything under the sun. She told me, she'd began looking for a job. As much as I wanted to protest, I couldn't. I had a decent amount of money saved up, but I knew we couldn't live off that forever. I didn't know when I would get another job, hell I hadn't even thought about filling out applications. I was just glad, I was making up for lost time that I'd missed by being in the army. When it got time for dessert, I contemplated on telling Quinn about my diagnosis and that I thought about going to see a therapist.

"I have something to tell you," I blurted out as I sat our slices of cheesecake on the table.

"I have something to tell you too. Maybe you should go first," Quinn responded.

When she said that I thought of everything negative she could possibly tell me and felt myself becoming upset. Instead of allowing that emotion to take over me, I tried my best to push that to the side and focus on telling her what I needed her to hear.

"Okay, so for a few months now, I have been discharged from the army. The reason is that—I was diagnosed with schizophrenia," I struggled to say.

Quinn's expression was hard to read, and I panicked because I didn't know how she would respond.

"Why didn't you tell me sooner? We could have started going to therapy, trying to work on fixing this," She responded and reached for my hand.

"Baby, to be honest, I was ashamed. I didn't know how to tell you. I didn't know how to go from having an almost normal life to living with a mental illness."

"I understand but you could have come to me sooner and we could have worked on this. I mean we still can, this will only make us stronger. We're going to get through this, believe me."

A smile crept on my face and I moved my chair closer to hers. I held her hand in mine and kissed it.

"Quinn, this is why I love you. You don't judge me, and you are always riding for me and caring. I'm sorry for everything I've ever caused you. I don't mean to be this way, but I can't help it, it's like something takes over me and I'm a different person," I confessed.

Quinn's eyes misted over. I was being honest with her. Quinn, I knew she'd be by my side and that I could count on her, no matter what. She reached over and caressed my cheek. I kissed her palm and slowly moved up to her arm. She was my rock, I was determined to make sure the things I'd done to her in the past, wouldn't continue. In my mind, I knew she deserved more than what I was giving her.

I was close to her face, so I grabbed her neck and moved her closer to place my lips on hers. Her mouth opened and invited my tongue into hers. Quinn kissed me like she wanted me like she was craving me, so I decided to do exactly what her body was asking of me. I stopped kissing her and grabbed her by the hands to stand her up. I swooped her up in my arms like I was carrying her across the threshold and walked upstairs.

Once in the bedroom, I placed her feet on the floor, kneeled, and began to take her shoes off. Next, I stood behind her, unzipped her dress, and watched it fall. Her perfectly shaped ass swallowed a black, lace thong. I couldn't help but snatch it off hungrily. I wanted what my wife was providing. She looked at me with hunger in her eyes, something I hadn't seen in a while because I'd been so busy smashing Erica. I stood in front of my naked wife, slowly came out of my clothes, and watched as her eyes dropped to my dick, that was pointing up at her.

She smirked and began to kneel, but I stopped her by placing my hands on her shoulders. I shook my head, then nodded towards the bed. She obliged by walking over to the bed and laid on top with her legs spread wide, showing me her freshly shaved kitty. My mouth began to water as I watched her dip her fingers inside of her wetness.

After taking her fingers out, she opened her mouth and sucked them like it was my dick. I looked down at my penis and couldn't understand why or how my piece could be so damn hard. I grabbed Quinn's legs, dragged her to the edge of the bed and got on my knees. I nuzzled my face in her hot box and took in her sweet scent. My tongue found her clit and moved across it causing her back to arch and soft moans to escape her lips. My face was coated with her juices and her legs were shaking like she was having a seizure.

"You ready for this dick, baby?" I asked looking into her eyes.

"I've been ready," Quinn responded.

A smirk appeared on my face as I guided my dick into her awaiting juice box. Her pussy gripped my dick and found the comfort of her G-spot as I began to pound away. My wife's pussy was different from Erica's and could make me cum instantly. Somehow, it takes me forever to cum with, Erica. I took my mind off the comparison's, looked down, and watched as she made love faces. I kissed her lips before I balanced myself on my knees and put her legs on my shoulders. Almost immediately, she began to squirt and yelled out for me to fuck her harder.

The beast in me came out as I rolled her onto her stomach. Her ass was in the air and I pinned her shoulders to the bed. I raised up on the balls of my feet and dug into her pussy like it was the last bit I was going to give her. Her hair was intertwined in my hands as I tugged at it and fucked her as hard as I could.

"You want to get fucked like this, hmm?" I asked.

"Ooh, yes—just like that!" Quinn yelled.

After each stroke, her juiciness was loud in my ears and her pussy queefed just a tad and made me excited. I felt myself getting ready to nut, but Quinn told me to let her up and for me to lay down. As I laid on my back, Quinn stood over me, slowly lowered her body over mine and eased my dick inside of her. She placed her hands on my chest and balanced herself on the balls of her feet. Quinn winked at me, then began bouncing up and down on my stick, while squeezing her vagina muscles every time she went up. My nut built back up again and I grabbed her by the waist causing her to stay still, while I thrust into her. Quinn threw her head back and squirted all over me, herself, and the bed.

"Ooh, Jason, yes—God," Quinn expressed.

I let my seed leak inside of her until my balls were drained and my toes were throwing up gang signs. Quinn rolled off top of me and laid down out of breath. Just then I remembered she had something to tell me.

"Baby what was it you had to tell me?" I asked moving her hair from her face.

"Oh, yeah, I forgot all about that."

"If it's something bad I don't want to hear it, right now."

"I'm pregnant."

"What—girl, how you know that? I just unloaded in you."

Quinn giggled and said, "No, that's why I went to the doctor this morning. I haven't had my period in two months."

"Are you serious?" I asked sitting straight up.

My heart pounded in my chest as I grew excited.

"Yes, I am."

I jumped from the bed and began doing a happy dance like the one *'Tyrese'* did in *'Baby Boy'*. Quinn laid on the bed laughing and at that moment, I knew things were going to get better. This was a sign, I was going to clearly accept. There would be better days.

~Quinn~

"I can't do this," I cried as I sat across the table talking with Kareem.

He'd invited me out for lunch while Jason decided to go handle some business and see his doctor about what he needed to do to get ahold of his illness.

"What do you mean you can't do this? Quinn, you have openly spoken about having kids, so what do you mean?" Kareem asked as he cut into his grilled steak.

"You are his friend, you gonna tell me, you didn't know why he was discharged from the army?" I asked.

"I didn't know. It was none of my business. I figured once he wanted somebody to know, he would let them."

I took a sip of my water and said, "Our relationship is all fucked up. He's abusive and now I find out that he was diagnosed with a mental illness. I cannot bring a child into a relationship like this."

"So, what are you going to do, Quinn?"

"Abortion is my only option. He's putting his hands on me and there is no way, I can allow him to do this to my child as well."

Kareem looked at me with sadness in his eyes. he grabbed my hand. "Quinn, I know this may be wrong, but I've grown to care for you in ways that I know for sure would end Jason and I's friendship. Abortion isn't the answer after I think things through, I can see about getting a transfer to any place you choose. We can take care of the baby together," he replied.

A smile spread across my face because I knew Kareem was genuine and meant what he said. I had to admit that, I did develop feelings for Kareem. I knew it was wrong because not only was he Jason's friend, but I was still in love with Jason and felt like I hadn't given him my all in attempting to fix our relationship.

"Kareem, you, already know what I'm going to say that. I know you mean it, but, right now I need you as a friend. This may not make sense to you, but before I make any moves, I want to make sure, I have my ducks in a row. It's not like Jason and I are in a regular relationship. We are married, and things can be a little more difficult."

Kareem smirked at me just a tad and returned to eating his food. His response was heartfelt, "Okay, Quinn, I'll be your friend."

"Good. Now that, that's out of the way, I hope you aren't busy next Thursday."

"I don't think I have anything to do. Why what's up?"

"I have an appointment, I need—"

Kareem cut me off by dropping his utensils. "I won't support that Quinn. You are going to have to take Erica for that one," he replied.

Without notice, my eyes began to tear up. I never told anyone how I suspected Jason and Erica were fucking around. I didn't have any proof, but I was going to have some soon. But right now, I was dealing with my heart breaking just at the slightest thought.

"Kareem, I can't take Erica with me. After that whole shit that went down at Denny's, things just ain't been the same. Not to mention, I think Jason is cheating on me with, Erica. I don't have any proof yet, but I feel it in my bones."

"Don't worry yourself about it if you don't have the proof. Take it with a grain of salt, when you have the proof then bring it up. That's how most women be looking dumb in the end, because they don't have proof," Kareem said, dismissing it with a wave of his hand.

My stomach was upset about the whole thing and I couldn't finish my food. I had the waiter wrap my food to go. I placed my portion of the meal ticket on the table top and rushed out leaving Kareem there. At that moment, all I wanted was be alone. My mind was made up and this abortion was going to happen one way or another.

I made my way home before Jason could make it home. I went into our bedroom, searched the closet, our dresser drawers, and under the bed, to see if I could find anything that would give me just the slightest clue that Jason was cheating on me. I found none, so I just gave up. Defeated, I sat on the bed and wondered what my life had come to. Never in a million years did I think, I would be going to get an abortion. Since I could remember, I always wanted kids, but then again when I was dreaming of having kids. I was in a healthy relationship and the man I was married to, adored me. He didn't put his hands on me. I was reliving my momma's relationship with my father and it wasn't a good thing.

This left me with no other choice, I got down on my knees in front of the bed and interlocked my fingers. I bowed my head and prayed that God would show me a way out of this relationship. I asked God to forgive me for the sin I was going to commit by killing my unborn child. I prayed until my knees were red and my body was shaking. I knew it was God's arms wrapping around me and protecting me. I just needed to get through Thursday and deal with things as they come.

***

~Thursday~

The rain was coming down as if God was angry with the earth and decided to wreak havoc on us with this horrible thunderstorm. My appointment was for one in the afternoon, I still had enough time to get ready. During the week, I was waiting for this day to arrive, Kareem tried to talk me out of it, but my mind was made up. I was going through with it. Jason hadn't come home last night, I'd tried to reach him before I left. Instead, I sent him a text message, explaining to him I was going to be stepping out for a few, and I left a note on the kitchen counter.

The thunder roared as I climbed into my car and made my way to Planned Parenthood, where I was going to be meeting Kareem. He was there when I arrived, waiting under an umbrella. When he saw me, he rushed over to me and opened my car door. A weak smile came across my face as we walked inside of the clinic together. My whole body shook as I filled out the necessary paperwork.

"You know, we can leave right now and forget about this day," Kareem said.

The room was packed with females from all walks of life.

"No, I didn't come this far to turn back now."

"Okay, at any time, you feel you want to run, just say the word."

I giggled and told him that I would. I needed one more favor from Kareem, but that would have to wait until I was done taking care of this situation. I started praying for my unborn and for God to protect his or her soul.

"Quinn Boyd," I heard my name being called as I ended my prayer. Kareem reached over and gave me a hug to let me know, he was here for me if I needed him. I squeezed his hand and walked with the nurse towards the back of the clinic. Once through the doors, I panicked and began to think, *'Was this a mistake?'*

~Erica~

Looking over to the opposite side of the bed, I watched as Jason slept, peacefully. I must have been crazy out of my mind to have thought about leaving his fine ass alone. Especially after he rocked this pussy into submission last night. Shit, if Quinn was willing we could all just be together and live as one big happy family. I kissed his sleeping lips, then decided I would make us a late breakfast. I'd already made my way to the grocery store. My plan was to wait until he woke up to cook, but I decided waking him up to it, would be a better idea.

I tossed around pots and pans and decided to make egg omelets, filled with diced ham, peppers, and onions, with hash browns, pancakes, and maple sausage patties. I made a big pot of coffee, placed everything on a tray, and walked to my room. Jason was laid out on his back, snoring loud enough to wake the dead. I sat the tray on the dresser and walked to the side of the bed where Jason was laying. A sneaky grin appeared on my face as I moved the covers away from his body. I licked my lips, pulled the elastic band from Jason's waistline and slid my hand inside to find his thickness. Slowly, I stroked him in hopes of waking the beast up. To no avail his dick limply flapped around in my hand, I decided to wet my lips and take him into my mouth. In just seconds, Jason grew inside my mouth and my eyes rolled to the back of my head at the feeling.

As soon as he felt the wetness of my mouth, I felt his fingers wrap around my hair, spit slid down the sides of my mouth as I smiled. Jason stopped my head from moving and pumped his dick in and out of my throat. That first-morning nut was approaching and I wanted it all. I looked up at Jason and tightened my jaws so he could bust down my throat. When he was ready his legs tightened, and he pulled his dick out of my mouth while rubbing it against my lips. His cum landed on my lips, forehead, hair, and eyelids.

"Ooh shit, fuck—damn, Quinn," Jason moaned out.

I shot up from the side of the bed, cum still on my face, surprised as hell. "Excuse me! What the fuck you just call me?"

Jason slowly opened his eyes and placed his dick back inside his boxers then he sat up. "Relax, I didn't call you by some regular bitch's name. It was my wife's," he responded.

I used the towel, I had hanging on the back of the door and wiped his kids from my face. Then I looked at Jason like he was crazy. "I don't give a shit if it's only your wife. When you with me, you with me," I expressed.

"Erica, you better calm your firecracker ass down. What did you cook? That shit smells good as fuck," he said.

I was so pissed off, the food that I'd just made went flying to the ground, as I knocked it off the dresser. How dare he act like it was okay? I went back and forth about whether I should kick him out, or if I should leave. Before I could leave out the room, Jason grabbed me by my hair stopping me in my tracks. He used all his strength, slung me to the floor, and stood over me with his fists clenched.

"Go ahead and hit me, you, punk ass bitch. But, keep in mind that while you are beating on me. I saw your wife going into Planned Parenthood with your best friend. I'm pretty sure, you know what goes down at Planned Parenthood, don't you?" It was a low blow, but I knew he wouldn't hit me if I used that against him. The look in his eyes went from anger to hurt and back to anger as he began to gather his things.

"Which one? And get your ass together cause you riding along. If she did what I think she did, I'm beating the shit out of both of you."

"Fuck, you, gonna hit me for? I didn't tell her dumb ass to get an abortion."

"You her friend ain't you?"

"The way I've been fucking her husband behind her back, I'd like to say, no I am not. So, all that putting your hands on me bullshit is dead," I spoke.

I grilled him as I fixed my hair and put my shoes on. His nostrils flared as he eyed me. I didn't care, I was built differently than Quinn, and there was no way in hell I was going to allow this nigga to put his hands on me. I grabbed my things, followed Jason to his car, and we made our way to the Planned Parenthood, on State Street and Brandywine Avenue. Jason rushed in once we got there, with me trailing behind.

"Hi, how can I help you, today?" The cheerful nurse asked as we approached the desk.

"I'm looking for my wife," Jason seethed as his jaw tightened.

"Okay, sir, what is her name?" She asked ready to type Quinn's name into the computer.

"Quinn Braxton."

The nurse typed her name into the computer and after a few seconds, she looked up shaking her head. "I'm sorry, we don't have that name in our system."

Jason's eyes got dark and he told her to try her maiden name. Low and behold, she was there and had been discharged thirty minutes before we'd arrived. Jason slammed his hand on the counter and yelled obscenities after the nurse told him, she couldn't verify what she was there for. Granted Planned Parenthood provided different services, but the main one was abortions. The pain that registered on Jason's face broke my heart. His eyes misted over, but he didn't allow any tears to drop.

"Maybe, she's home. Just drop me off and go deal with her. I'm gonna be here if you need me," I told him.

Jason didn't respond, he just nodded his head and drove me to my house. I felt bad I'd told him, and it wasn't for Quinn's sake, it was for his. When I arrived at my house, I kissed his cheek and went inside. I'd never seen him, so heartbroken, and I wished I could take it back.

Once inside of my house, I went straight to my room and cleaned up the mess I'd made. Once it was all cleaned up, my phone rang, taking me from out of my thoughts.

"Hello," I asked.

I knew it was Jason from the ringtone. He didn't say anything for a cool minute and I just let him sit there quietly until he was ready to talk.

"She's not here and some of her things are missing," he finally said, then, just hung up.

MIMI

Chapter Fourteen

Only God knows where the story is
For me, but I know where the story begins
It's up to us to choose
Whatever we win or lose
And I choose to win

Flashes of the past two hours ran through my mind. My white, porcelain, claw-foot tub held scorching hot water, awaiting my descend. I looked around the all-white bathroom and my eyes connected with the circular mirror, I had avoided for so many months. Slowly, my eyes began to wander up and settled on the person looking back at me. I didn't recognize her. My once flawless, light-honey colored skin was free from the foundation, I used daily to cover up the scars.

My eyes were swollen and bruised from the constant abuse, I'd suffered for the past two hours. Though, that didn't compare to the constant abuse I've experienced over the last few months. My lip was busted so bad it was split on the top and bottom. There was blood draining from my ear, down my face, and onto my shoulder. My hair, my thick, beautiful hair was now extremely thin due to stress and tossed around on my head.

If you would have asked me if I knew this was going to happen, I would have said no. In fact, I was outright angry at myself for allowing this to happen. As I looked at myself in the mirror, I forced myself to wipe the tears from my eyes deciding now was the perfect time to stop feeling sorry for myself. I took off the terry cloth robe and saw new black and blue bruises along with the yellow discoloration from the old ones. Tears threatened to fall from my eyes but I wouldn't allow them to do so. For years I'd cried, today was the day, I stopped and stood strong.

Finally turning from the mirror, I walked over to the tub and one foot after the other, I slid in. The water sloshed around my body threatening to spill over, but it immediately soothed my aching body. In flashes, I remembered the backhanded slap I received from Jason, the pain from the punch that landed to my stomach, and the words, *"You, worthless piece of shit!"* rang through my head. I shut my eyes as tight as I could to get rid of those thoughts. The room was silent, so silent I couldn't bear it.

The sound of heels clicking across the marble, tiled floors outside the bathroom caught my attention. My ears perked up as I listened to the high heels crackle over the glass that lined the floor in the hallway. In walked my best friend of seventeen years. Her mouth was agape, and her eyes bugged out of her head, once she laid her eyes on me. I stared back at her with the silence that needed to happen. I knew she couldn't believe the severity of the issue at hand, and she was in complete utter shock. Slowly, Erica began walking towards me and sat on the toilet.

"Quinn, baby girl, what happened?" Erica asked.

It was obvious what had happened, but I guess when you're in shock you ask the obvious.

I looked at Erica and exhaled through the pain I felt in my ribs. "I ended a cycle," I said.

Erica looked down at me, while I was in the tub with disgust written on her face. "What did you do to him, Quinn? Did you kill him, where is he at?" she asked.

I realized I wouldn't be able to relax, without answering Erica. I made my way out of the tub, my body was in so much pain, I could barely stand. When Erica realized I wasn't going to answer her question, she walked out of the bathroom, more than likely to search for Jason. I chuckled, shook my head, and slowly slipped on my bra and panties, sweatpants, T-shirt, socks, and shoes. Then I grabbed some tissue and tried to wipe as much blood off my face as I could. The pain was unbearable. I walked into the spare room, where I had left an unconscious, Jason. Erica was standing over him weeping and trying to wake him up.

"Jason, baby, you got to wake up," she cried.

"I didn't kill him," I said.

Erica's body stiffened as her back was turned to me. "You, stupid bitch," Erica roared as she stood to her feet and prepared to charge me.

The gun that was in my hands stopped her in her tracks. The color drained from her face as her eyes went from my face to the gun.

"I should have listened to my gut a while ago. You were supposed to be my friend, Erica, fuck that, you were my sister. We've been through thick and thin together. How could you do this?"

"It was just something that happened, Quinn. I told Jason that this was something we needed to stop, but he insisted that we continue."

A maddening laugh slipped through my lips. "You just gonna stand there and act like you was innocent in this? I'm not stupid, Erica. You forget I used to run with you through these streets. You forget I had to save you a time or two from almost getting your ass beat by nigga's wives? You have everything to do with it just as much as Jason does. So, blaming just him instant going to work," I snapped.

Erica's attitude changed as she took on a nonchalant demeanor and folded her arms across her chest. Was she being serious, right now? I lowered my hand and shook my head. Although, everything in my body wanted to put a bullet in them both, but decided it wasn't worth it. The last two hours played in my head in flashes and hurt more than the physical pain.

~Two Hours Before~

Being gone for two days allowed me to get my thoughts and mind together. After coming so close to getting an abortion and going against what I believed in. I asked Kareem to take me to a hotel. He asked me what happened when I went inside the room after the nurse called me back. Simply, I told him, I couldn't go through with it. Even though my child's father was the devil's spawn, I was going to love him or her no matter what. My mind was made up and I had decided to leave Jason to at least give my child the chance to grow up happily.

After several calls, text messages, and voicemails from Jason over the last two days, I decided to face the music. I knew Jason was going to be pissed, but more than likely, he was going to have to listen to what I had to say. At least that's what I thought.

"You want me to come in with you?" Kareem asked.

Thinking about it, I shook my head. Kareem had done enough for me, and I was pretty sure I could handle Jason. I told Kareem to go home and get some rest, and I would call him if I needed him. I knew he was hesitant, but I assured him that I would be fine. Kareem reluctantly agreed to go home. I climbed out of Kareem's car and waved at him once I got to the door. Upon entering my home, there was an odor that hit me like a ton of bricks. The heat was on hell, which it didn't need to be because for it to be March, it was warm outside.

The smell led me into the kitchen where there was garbage overflowing from the bin and spilling onto the floor. The freezer door was wide open which caused the meat to spoil because the heat was too high in the house. I shook my head, closed the freezer, and grabbed a garbage bag from the pantry that was next to the fridge. As I cleaned up the kitchen, I wondered where Jason was. His car was in the driveway, but he hadn't made himself visible yet. Ten minutes later, the garbage was fixed and outside as well as the spoiled meat.

Taking my ass upstairs, I noticed that Jason wasn't in the room either. Thankfully, I exhaled, grabbed a suitcase from the closet and began to pack it. 'Maybe I won't have to deal with him' I thought. While I busied myself packing for ten minutes, I didn't realize Jason was leaning against the door. I was ankle deep in clothes trying to decide what to take and what to leave.

"You going, somewhere?" Jason's voice boomed from behind me, causing me to jump out of my skin.

I looked over my shoulder, Jason was standing there with a glass of dark liquid in his hand. I knew just where he had been. In the basement, we'd put a bar down there a few months prior, and judging from the smell coming from him, he had to have been down there for a while. I rubbed my hands against my pants and looked at Jason.

"Um, Jason—" I began.

"Um, Jason my ass! Where the hell have you been for the last two days?"

"I needed time to think, so I got a room."

"You have a house for that. I got your note, where did you go?"

I took a seat on the bed and looked at Jason.

'Should I tell him, I'd come close to aborting our child? Or do I just think up a quick lie to try and get him off my back?' I thought. "Two days ago, I went to Planned Parenthood but when I got there—"

"You got rid of my child, huh! How could you do this to me?" Jason spat with hurt in his voice.

He stood over me with his fists balled at his side. My whole body shook in fear as my chin tucked into my chest and tears slid down my face.

"Jason, I—" without letting me get another word, Jason with his hand opened, slapped me in my face so hard I fell off the bed and my ear instantly started ringing.

"You had the nerve to go and get rid of my child with my best friend! Was that his baby and y'all were trying to hide it from me?" he yelled.

I was curled up in the corner, covering my body as Jason used his fists to express the way he'd been feeling. It didn't help that he didn't even let me explain.

"Jason, stop, you're hurting me!" I screeched.

"You, hurt me first," Was all he said as he dragged me by the ankles into the bathroom.

He grabbed me by the arm and threw me into the bathtub.

"Jason, please, just listen to me!"

Unexpectedly, Jason drew his hand back and punched me in the mouth, causing my tooth to get lodged in my bottom lip splitting it. Blood leaked from my mouth and I saw white spots forming in my eyes.

"When I get back, you need to be undressed. To say that I was confused was an understatement. I thought of our unborn child and a part of me felt regret, as I thought about not going through with it. Tears ran down my face like a downpour, as I stood up to take my clothes off. It didn't make sense to me but the look in Jason's eyes told me, I'd better listen. In my mind, I thought of so many ways I could be leaving out of this house, but fear kept me still.

Jason came back to the bathroom and turned the shower water on cold while I stood there shivering, wondering why he was running the cold water on me. I dared not to ask. That crazy look told me I shouldn't. Even though I decided not to ask, I still tried to reason with him, to get him to listen to me.

"Jason, please, I—I need you to listen to me," I shook while saying.

Jason eyed me with a tight face. We held our gaze for a while and I thought he was going to let me explain. That was until the sting on my skin cause me to yell out in pain. This man done lost his mind if he thought he was going to beat me with a belt like I was a child. Trying to dodge the belt, Jason lashed me across my stomach and then grabbed me by the arm, dragging me from the shower. Halfway down the hallway, he dropped me to the ground and continued to beat me with the belt. My whole body was red and full of welts.

"I took your ass out of the hood, took care of you, fed you, clothed you, and you repay me by killing my seed?" Jason threw the belt, climbed over me, and wrapped his hands around my neck. "I should kill you in this, bitch, Quinn! I fucking love you and was trying to change to be a better man for you. And you thank me by killing my child," he fumed.

My fingers scraped and clawed at his hands as I tried to get them from around my neck. His hands were wrapped so tightly around my neck, I couldn't even make the sound like I was gasping for air. Jason's eyes were so dark, I could tell the Jason I knew had clocked out. I didn't know who this was. Slowly my eyes rolled to the back of my head, I knew, I was close to giving up. God had other plans though because Jason got up from over me and the air became my best friend.

"If – you – would – just – listen – to – me," I gasped and cried at the same time.

Jason didn't speak, he balled up his fist and hit me as hard as he could. My eye swelled almost immediately. Jason kicked me and walked away.

'Lord please help me out of this. Please protect my baby until I can get to those doors.' I prayed silently.

Enough was enough, I was humiliated because of Jason beating me while I was wet like a child. I looked around for Jason, I noticed he wasn't anywhere near me, so I began to crawl towards the stairs. Jason's feet thundered behind me as I tried to move faster towards the stairs.

"Oh no, you not going anywhere!" Jason shouted, grabbing me by the ankles and dragging me.

We got back to the bedroom where he lifted me up and tried to throw me onto the bed but missed completely. I rolled off the bed and landed on the floor with a thud. My head banged against the floor, dazing me. Jason rushed over and in no time, his fists were connecting with my body. No matter how hard I screamed and yelled, it went unheard. Two minutes later, Jason stopped, but I believe it was only because he was winded. I laid on the floor crying and hyperventilating. To add insult to injury, Jason raised his foot and stomped right on my stomach while yelling something about if I killed his child, I wouldn't be able to carry kids for anyone else.

'At least he knows after this I will be leaving his ass,' I thought.

Jason walked out of the room leaving me by myself once again. This time, I planned on doing something when he came back. I didn't know where I got the strength to put on some sweats, a shirt, and some beat – a – bitch – ass Timbs. I sat on the bed with my back facing the door, the lamp that was on the nightstand was in between my legs, and I was struggling to breathe.

"I thought, I told you, you weren't going nowhere. But you got dressed, anyway," Jason said sinisterly.

His steps grew closer and as soon as I thought he was close enough, I hoisted the lamp up and smashed it right into his face, causing him to fall to the floor immediately. As soon as he dropped to the floor, I stood over him and looked down at him. His face now matched mine and without a second thought, I climbed over him and proceeded to punch him in the face. All my frustrations were being released.

"If you would have let me explain, you would have known that I didn't get the abortion. But thanks to you, I'm probably going to miscarry and never have a chance to carry another child! I fucking hate you, Jason!" I yelled.

My God it felt good to let it all out. Feeling winded, I got up and without grabbing anything but my phone, I texted Kareem to come back fast. Making my way towards the stairs again, I stopped at the bathroom to grab a wash rag. I wet it with cold water and patted it on my face. As I returned to the hallway, a smile spread across my face because I smelled freedom.

"Aahhh," I heard from behind me.

When I turned around, Jason was coming at me full speed. I was shook and couldn't move in enough time, next thing I knew he pushed me. Instantly, I thought of my mother's death and fear filled me. This was not how I wanted to go out. After stumbling, trying to find something to grab onto, knocking pictures off the wall, I finally fell and landed on my face.

Jason turned me onto my back and climbed over me. As I saw his hands coming towards my neck again, I swiftly kicked him in his nuts and he instantly folded like a bitch. I'd be damned if he was going to put his hands on me again without me putting up a fight. I was leaving this fucked up relationship, marriage, or whatever the hell you wanted to call it.

"You don't know when to get enough, do you? I'm not going to keep playing this game with you!" I was done with this and I only knew one way he would stop.

I marched into the spare bedroom and began rummaging through the closet. I grabbed what I was looking for, closed the closet and saw Jason standing by the doorway. We stared at each other, he was probably contemplating his next move and truth be told, seeing his eye twitch, I knew he'd made up his mind. He prepared himself to charge and as he got closer, I moved out of the way in the nick of time, causing him to stumble and on his way down, he banged his head against the radiator and with a reflex, I fired the gun I was holding and shot him in his leg. He laid there not moving, with a shrug of my shoulders, I walked back into my room to grab an outfit to change into.

Kareem texted me back and said he'd be here in fifteen minutes. I was pretty sure Jason was going to be out for a while, so I decided on soaking in the tub for five minutes. After looking in the mirror for some time, I placed the gun on the toilet under my clothes, by the tub. Just in case he decided to come in and act up again. Then Erica walked into the chaos.

***

"You know you are going to go to jail for shooting him? I'm going to make sure, he presses charges against you!" Erica yelled at my back.

The house door opening, and closing caught my attention, but the sound of Kareem's voice relaxed me.

I looked at Erica and said, "You were supposed to be my sister and you're choosing this nigga, a nigga who ain't even yours, over somebody who has had your back this whole time, through everything. And you do this to me? You think this nigga gonna treat you like gold once I'm out of the picture? You better think again, because the exact same thing he did to me, he's gonna do to you. But the funny thing is, I just hope you get out of it sooner than I did. Love does hurt, and I pray that you don't fall and that you learn from my mistakes."

There was nothing left to say after that, so I threw up the deuces and made my way towards the stairs to meet Kareem at the bottom.

Erica followed me and yelled, "Quinn, you can't just walk away. Let's talk about this!"

"You should have thought about that before you decided to throw your hoe ass pussy on my nigga's dick! I'm good love, enjoy!"

Kareem was standing at the bottom of the stairs waiting for me, but his back was turned.

"I'm ready to go," I said with my hands in my pockets.

Kareem turned to face me, and his reaction was of shock, then anger.

"Where the fuck is he?" Kareem growled.

He began to walk past me, but I grabbed him by his arm to stop him.

"Kareem, it's not worth it. We can fight this another way."

"Are you sure?"

"Yes, I am. Just take me to the hospital so we can begin this process."

Kareem pulled me in for a hug and did the unthinkable. He lifted my chin and kissed my lips. No tongue, just a simple kiss of passion. "I will be there for you every step of the way. I promise you, on my life, you will never have to deal with this type of pain ever again. Let's go," he assured.

~The End~
Crime of Passion 2
Coming Soon

If you or anyone that you know is being subjected to abuse, speak up and speak out by calling the Domestic Violence Hotline at 1-800-799-7233 (SAFE)
You are a survivor!

Submission Guideline.

Submit the first three chapters of your completed manuscript to ldpsubmissions@gmail.com, subject line: Your book's title. The manuscript must be in a .doc file and sent as an attachment. Document should be in Times New Roman, double spaced and in size 12 font. Also, provide your synopsis and full contact information. If sending multiple submissions, they must each be in a separate email.

Have a story but no way to send it electronically? You can still submit to LDP/Ca$h Presents. Send in the first three chapters, written or typed, of your completed manuscript to:

LDP: Submissions Dept
Po Box 870494
Mesquite, Tx 75187

DO NOT send original manuscript. Must be a duplicate.

Provide your synopsis and a cover letter containing your full contact information.

Thanks for considering LDP and Ca$h Presents.

Coming Soon from Lock Down Publications/Ca$h Presents

BOW DOWN TO MY GANGSTA

By **Ca$h**

TORN BETWEEN TWO

By **Coffee**

BLOOD STAINS OF A SHOTTA **III**

By **Jamaica**

WHEN THE STREETS CLAP BACK **III**

By **Jibril Williams**

STEADY MOBBIN

By **Marcellus Allen**

BLOOD OF A BOSS **V**

By **Askari**

LOYAL TO THE GAME **IV**

By **T.J. & Jelissa**

A DOPEBOY'S PRAYER **II**

By **Eddie "Wolf" Lee**

IF LOVING YOU IS WRONG… **III**

LOVE ME EVEN WHEN IT HURTS

By **Jelissa**

TRUE SAVAGE **V**

By **Chris Green**

TRAPHOUSE KING **III**

By **Hood Rich**

BLAST FOR ME **III**

By **Ghost**

ADDICTIED TO THE DRAMA **III**

MIMI

By **Jamila Mathis**

LIPSTICK KILLAH **III**

CRIME OF PASSION **II**

By **Mimi**

WHAT BAD BITCHES DO **III**

THE BOSS MAN'S DAUGHTERS **V**

By **Aryanna**

THE COST OF LOYALTY **II**

By **Kweli**

SHE FELL IN LOVE WITH A REAL ONE **II**

By **Tamara Butler**

LOVE SHOULDN'T HURT **II**

By **Meesha**

CORRUPTED BY A GANGSTA **III**

By **Destiny Skai**

A GANGSTER'S CODE II

By **J-Blunt**

KING OF NEW YORK

By **T.J. Edwards**

CUM FOR ME **IV**

By **Ca$h & Company**

Available Now

RESTRAINING ORDER **I & II**

By **CA$H & Coffee**

LOVE KNOWS NO BOUNDARIES **I II & III**

By **Coffee**

RAISED AS A GOON I, II, III & IV

176

CRIME OF PASSION
BRED BY THE SLUMS I, II, III

BLAST FOR ME I & II

By **Ghost**

LAY IT DOWN **I & II**

LAST OF A DYING BREED

BLOOD STAINS OF A SHOTTA I & II

By **Jamaica**

LOYAL TO THE GAME

LOYAL TO THE GAME II

LOYAL TO THE GAME III

By **TJ & Jelissa**

BLOODY COMMAS I & II

SKI MASK CARTEL I II & III

By **T.J. Edwards**

IF LOVING HIM IS WRONG…I & II

By **Jelissa**

WHEN THE STREETS CLAP BACK I & II

By **Jibril Williams**

A DISTINGUISHED THUG STOLE MY HEART I II & III

LOVE SHOULDN'T HURT

By **Meesha**

A GANGSTER'S CODE

By J-Blunt

PUSH IT TO THE LIMIT

By **Bre' Hayes**

BLOOD OF A BOSS **I, II, III & IV**

By **Askari**

THE STREETS BLEED MURDER **I, II & III**

THE HEART OF A GANGSTA I II& III

MIMI

By **Jerry Jackson**

CUM FOR ME

CUM FOR ME 2

CUM FOR ME 3

An **LDP Erotica Collaboration**

BRIDE OF A HUSTLA **I II & II**

THE FETTI GIRLS **I, II& III**

CORRUPTED BY A GANGSTA I & II

By **Destiny Skai**

WHEN A GOOD GIRL GOES BAD

By **Adrienne**

A GANGSTER'S REVENGE **I II III & IV**

THE BOSS MAN'S DAUGHTERS

THE BOSS MAN'S DAUGHTERS II

THE BOSSMAN'S DAUGHTERS III

THE BOSSMAN'S DAUGHTERS IV

A SAVAGE LOVE **I & II**

BAE BELONGS TO ME

A HUSTLER'S DECEIT I, II

WHAT BAD BITCHES DO I, II

By **Aryanna**

A KINGPIN'S AMBITON

A KINGPIN'S AMBITION **II**

I MURDER FOR THE DOUGH

By **Ambitious**

TRUE SAVAGE

TRUE SAVAGE II

TRUE SAVAGE **III**

TRUE SAVAGE **IV**

178

CRIME OF PASSION
By **Chris Green**

A DOPEBOY'S PRAYER

By **Eddie "Wolf" Lee**

THE KING CARTEL **I, II & III**

By **Frank Gresham**

THESE NIGGAS AIN'T LOYAL **I, II & III**

By **Nikki Tee**

GANGSTA SHYT **I II &III**

By **CATO**

THE ULTIMATE BETRAYAL

By **Phoenix**

BOSS'N UP **I , II & III**

By **Royal Nicole**

I LOVE YOU TO DEATH

By Destiny J

I RIDE FOR MY HITTA

I STILL RIDE FOR MY HITTA

By **Misty Holt**

LOVE & CHASIN' PAPER

By **Qay Crockett**

TO DIE IN VAIN

By **ASAD**

BROOKLYN HUSTLAZ

By **Boogsy Morina**

BROOKLYN ON LOCK I & II

By **Sonovia**

GANGSTA CITY

By **Teddy Duke**

A DRUG KING AND HIS DIAMOND I & II

MIMI
A DOPEMAN'S RICHES

By Nicole Goosby

TRAPHOUSE KING I & II

By **Hood Rich**

LIPSTICK KILLAH **I, II**

CRIME OF PASSION

By **Mimi**

BOOKS BY LDP'S CEO, CA$H

TRUST IN NO MAN

TRUST IN NO MAN 2

TRUST IN NO MAN 3

BONDED BY BLOOD

SHORTY GOT A THUG

THUGS CRY

THUGS CRY 2

THUGS CRY 3

TRUST NO BITCH

TRUST NO BITCH 2

TRUST NO BITCH 3

TIL MY CASKET DROPS

RESTRAINING ORDER

RESTRAINING ORDER 2

IN LOVE WITH A CONVICT

Coming Soon

BONDED BY BLOOD 2

BOW DOWN TO MY GANGSTA

MIMI

Made in the USA
Coppell, TX
15 March 2022

75038054R00105